Branson Hawk

U.S. Marshal

Book Two

Dead Man's

Gold

Randall Dale

Randall Dale

Dead Man's Gold

Randall Dale

ISBN: 9781088721001

Printed August 2019 in the

United States of America

Chapter 1

The rearmost Santa Fe Railroad company car swayed on the uneven rails and the constant clackity-clack of the wheels had long since been relegated to the furthermost recesses of my consciousness. In the unheated car, the February cold surrounded my shoulders and chest, pressing inward which made it difficult to breathe even though I wore my knee-length coat. I rested with my head against the side boards, my flat-brimmed hat pulled low, my arms folded and legs extended and crossed at the ankles. I swayed slightly with the movements of the train and though I appeared asleep, if anyone had been watching, they would have seen me occasionally cock my head to look out the window to the passing New Mexico countryside. I would be in Deming in another hour for an overnight stop then on to Benson in Arizona Territory the next day on the newly completed Southern Pacific Railroad.

I noticed the door open at the front of the car and a portly conductor in a rumpled, sweat-stained, once-white shirt entered and stood perusing each of the passengers. When he finally saw me, he staggered down the aisle, holding to the seat backs for balance. A beautiful, blonde woman in a heavy coat over a tight-necked black dress and matching hat with a veil followed unsteadily behind.

The conductor stopped when he reached my side. "Excuse me."

I sighed then pushed my hat higher on my head. It seemed as though no matter where I went people were always asking for my help, but, I supposed, that was to be expected because of the U. S. Marshal's badge pinned to my shirt. I glanced at the portly man, then my eyes rested on the woman. I had to refrain from staring. I nodded before focusing once again on the conductor. "Yes?"

"Pardon me sir, but I noticed the badge when you got on the train in Santa Fe."

I glanced again at the woman, allowing my gaze to linger. She averted her eyes, obviously uncomfortable at the scrutiny, so I rubbed my jaw then nodded encouragement for the conductor to continue.

A rough spot on the tracks caused the car to lurch to the left then immediately back to the right. The conductor, holding tightly to the seat backs, remained on his feet but the woman was less fortunate. She fell awkwardly toward the seat directly in front of me.

I jolted forward and caught her, then held her so she could ease into the bench seat. Embarrassed, she brushed the wrinkles from her dress and adjusted her hat.

"Thank you, Mr.—?"

"Hawk, ma'am. Branson Hawk, U. S. Marshal." I lightly touched the brim of my hat. "Pleased to make your acquaintance."

The conductor cleared his throat. "Miss Trudeau," he motioned toward the woman, "is the victim of a robbery."

I looked from the conductor to the lady. A robbery? Well, that was certainly more interesting than so many of the requests I received. Requests to find someone's long, lost brother or to help with filing a mining claim, registering a brand or serving court papers, or any other such mundane matters that the public too often felt I should be involved in.

I glanced back to her. "I see. Are you quite all right?"

"Yes. Thank you." Her eyes suddenly opened wide. "I was not accosted if that is what you're asking. But the evil man took my hand bag."

"Here on the train?"

"Yes. In the next car." She gestured vaguely with her hand.

I held the corner of my lip in my teeth, an inadvertent habit when I was thinking. "Did you see him take it?"

She shook her head and long, blonde ringlets danced around her face. "I held it on my lap then I must have gone to sleep. When I awoke it was gone."

"How can you be sure it was him?"

She grimaced and pulled her eyebrows low. "He sat across from me. The seat next to me was empty as was the seat next to him. He is such an uncouth man, placing his dirty boots next to me on the bench and staring at me like a hungry wolf. It was him all right. After I woke up, I noticed my handbag was gone and when I started looking for it he pulled his shirt more tightly around his chest, but he wasn't fast enough. I saw my handbag inside his shirt."

I stared at her face and wondered for a moment if my own expression was that of a hungry wolf. She was extraordinarily beautiful, even in the black mourning gown. But enough of that, I decided, because I simply didn't have the time.

"Did you confront him?"

Her expression of exasperation pained me and I acknowledged to myself that perhaps it had been an ill-advised question. What should she have done, threaten to physically take it from the thief?

"Of course not! How could I? My only chance to get it back was to allow him to think he'd gotten away with the theft. I asked the conductor for help and he led me to you."

I nodded toward her, a gesture of remorse for the question. "Well, I'm glad you did Miss Trudeau." I focused on the conductor. "Do you know of the man she is describing? Can you point him out to me?"

The conductor puffed his chest in exaggerated self-importance. "I believe so. Miss Trudeau came and found me then together we came to find you. I suspect he doesn't know there is a U. S. Marshal on the train, or that we have come to ask for your assistance."

I glanced to the woman again. The train would be in Deming in less than an hour so I rose from my seat and hitched my Colt .45 on my hip. With a snap, I pulled the lapels of my broadcloth coat.

I pointed to the seat. "You stay here, ma'am. I'll see what I can do." I motioned for the conductor to lead the way.

In the forward car, a big man in dirty clothes and a floppy, greasy, felt hat watched us approach. I glanced at the conductor and got a nod of confirmation that this was indeed the accused man. I tugged one more time at the lapels of my coat then stepped forward.

"Is this seat taken?" I pointed to the bench seat next to the muddy boots, the seat Miss Trudeau had obviously used.

The big man sneered. "A lady's been sittin' there. Go find yourself another bench."

A well-oiled and cared for handgun rested easily in a holster high on the man's hip and it looked like it had been used aplenty. I saw it and knew immediately that it wasn't there for decoration. I would need to keep the upper hand so acting as though I hadn't heard, I stepped over the big man's legs and plopped into the empty seat.

The thief sat up quickly and his heavy, mud-caked boots clunked loudly to the wooden floor. "Hey. Didn't you hear what I said?"

"I heard."

I leaned forward and without warning, viciously slapped the beefy face, then, gripping his shirt, I jerked the big man forward. The thief, dazed by the suddenness and intensity of the attack, shook his head in disbelief for only an instant, then he lashed out, but he was too slow. I threw him back against the seat then drove a hard right to his heart then a left to the throat causing instantaneously tight and labored gasps for air.

In less than a heartbeat, the business end of my gun pressed lightly against the big man's upper lip. With eyes wide open, the thief sank back, all the fight gone.

I nodded and awarded the man a cold-blooded smile. "Now, Mister, I have it on good authority that you have a woman's handbag stuffed inside your shirt."

Three buttons popped when I jerked his shirt open. They dropped, clickity-clacking to the floor. As expected, the handbag rested against a hairy chest. I lifted it away, then with intentional severity, rapped the barrel of my gun against the man's lip. A crunching sound of a breaking tooth could be heard immediately before the scream. I released my grip and he slumped in his seat and buried his face in his hands.

It was over almost before it started. I stood, ignoring the expressions of shock on the faces of a few of the nearby passengers—or the nods of approval from others. For a moment I thought of taking the man into custody, but dismissed the idea as the jails were always full to overflowing in Deming. Besides, I had the handbag, which I would return to Miss Trudeau, and the criminal had been duly punished, Branson Hawk style. The man would live the rest of his miserable life missing one or possibly both of his front teeth. In a deliberate motion, I replaced my own pistol then retrieved the one from his holster and opened the cylinder. Holding the gun upside down, I allowed the bullets to slip out one by one and bounce on the floor. When empty, I flipped the cylinder back into place and casually tossed the gun to the empty bench.

I leaned close to his ear. "In the future you might want to think twice about taking what doesn't belong to you."

Blood dribbled from the thief's mouth and cut lip as he looked up into my face. "I'll kill you for this."

I smiled without humor, then waved my hand dismissively. "Better men than you have tried." I stepped to the aisle and backed away holding to the seats. I knew better than to turn my back, for the man might have another gun or a knife. I'd known of lawmen who'd been killed that way and it wasn't a chance I was willing to take.

When I finally turned, I walked quickly, then slipped through the doors and into the last car where the beautiful woman waited. She sat facing away in the same seat where I'd left her. She turned at the sound of my boots on the hardwood floor.

She stood and with a nod, I handed her the handbag. She took it and held it to her chest with a grateful smile.

"Thank you, Marshal."

"My pleasure, ma'am." I pointed to the bench, inviting her to sit. "Would you care to join me for the last few minutes of the trip?"

She smiled and took the seat. I did the same.

I cocked my head and stared at her beautiful face behind the thin, black veil. "My condolences."

She looked away and shook her head. "I'm coming from Santa Fe to take my brother back home for burial. He was killed in a mining accident in Benson." She brought her kerchief to her face to wipe her eyes under the veil. "I got the telegraph message yesterday. I can't believe he's gone."

I perked up at the mention of Benson because that was my destination also. I nodded. "Benson is where I'm heading. The train will leave Deming tomorrow morning and we'll be there sometime after noon. Might I be so bold as to offer my assistance?"

She returned her hands and kerchief to her lap and smiled bravely. "So kind of you to volunteer. I'd be delighted to travel together. How fortunate to have met you."

I glanced at her face, thinking I was the fortunate one.

Neither of us spoke for a few minutes. She held her kerchief on her lap and nervously picked at her fingernails. As she came to realize what she was doing, she sighed in exasperation and looked at me again. "Is your trip to Benson official business?"

I smiled. "It is." I would have liked to have told her more just to keep the conversation going. Truth be told, my reason for a visit to Benson was nothing more than to remind a man about his testimony at an upcoming trial, then I would be off to my home in Tucson. Still, I'd made it a practice never to talk of my cases and that choice had served me well. I pushed my hat back on my head and glanced at her with my head cocked. I hoped she would continue and I was happy that she did.

She nodded. "Is it a quiet place?"

I grinned. "Nobody could accuse Benson, Arizona of being a quiet place. Until a few years ago it was a tiny town with a livery, a telegraph office, a saloon and an eatery, but when the railroad approached, and with it the hundreds of railroad workers, the town exploded. Last I heard there were seven saloons and two more getting ready to open."

She wrinkled her nose in thought. "Wouldn't the railroad workers have moved on as the tracks were laid toward the next town?" She leaned closer. "That happened all over Northern New Mexico. The railroad towns would boom, then within only a few months the track stretched out and the workers would be off to the next location."

I chuckled at her astute observation. She obviously was a woman who paid attention. "I suppose that could have been the case with Benson, but the mines within freighting distance kept it from going bust. There is a small smelter there where many of the mines ship their ore to be processed."

The cars jerked and steam billowed as the train approached the Deming station. Men and women on the train stood as soon as it stopped, gathering their belongings and making hasty exits onto the station platform so they could get on their way to various destinations in town. I had only a small satchel, which I placed under one arm, then I held out my hand for the woman.

"Do you have any luggage?"

She took my hand and stood, then pulled her coat more closely around her shoulders. She ran a gloved hand under the lace at her throat. "Only one bag. It was checked in Santa Fe and should be in the baggage car. I'll have it delivered to the hotel."

"Very good." I found myself staring again. "I'll escort you as far as the hotel?"

"You are so kind. Thank you."

I got off the train then helped her onto the busy platform. A cold wind swirled through the station so we both pulled our coats, and although I was anxious to find a windbreak, I took a moment to look through the crowd to see if the man with the broken tooth might be searching for me. A U. S. Marshal didn't get to be thirty-four by taking unnecessary chances after being threatened. There was no sign of the man so arm in arm, Miss Trudeau and I hurried to the station office so she could arrange for her bag to be delivered. That done, we made our way to the biggest hotel in town, the Hatch House, where we registered and were given keys, her to room seven and me to room twelve.

I escorted her up the stairs and to her room.

"Thank you, Mr. Hawk."

"My pleasure, I'm sure." I waited until the door closed then I strolled to my room down the hall.

Once inside I poured water from the pitcher into the basin and washed my face. While drying I studied my reflection in the mirror. I'd been told I was handsome. Maybe I was and maybe I wasn't, it didn't much matter to me one way or the other. I rubbed the four days of whiskers on my face and saw my hair curling over my ears. I pulled my pocket watch and clicked open the lid. Four o'clock. I smiled to myself at the recollection of seeing a barbershop on our way from the depot to the hotel. I had plenty of time to get a shave and haircut before supper. If I was to travel with a beautiful woman, I decided I'd best look presentable.

The wind howled through town and when I opened the door to the one-chair barbershop under the main-street veranda, I had to hold it tightly to keep it from blowing so far open that it might break. I stepped inside and pulled the door closed behind me. The barber, an older, white-haired man with round spectacles stood from a bench while carefully folding a newspaper and placing it on a table.

"Welcome."

I nodded. "Shave and a haircut?"

He glanced at my badge then smiled and gestured to the chair in the middle of the room. He maneuvered the chair, leaning it back until I was almost prone, then he shook a large cloth and covered me from my chin to my knees. I closed my eyes and relaxed and could hear the pleasant swishing of the brush in the cup as he mixed the foam. Within a minute he'd lathered my face and with rhythmic slapping, worked the razor against the strap.

Without words, he went to work and I was happy that he didn't expect any conversation. One of the pleasures I enjoyed in life was getting a shave, but I always enjoyed doing so in quiet. I despised barbers who felt like they needed to talk the whole time, or worse, those that expected me to join in the conversation.

When he finished the left side, I got nervous, as I always did, as he started on my throat, but he competently finished and moved to the right side.

Suddenly the door flew open and as it caught the wind, it crashed with a terrible noise. Cold wind rushed through the shop and the newspaper, so carefully folded by the barber at my entry, leapt from the table and swirled noisily about the room. From my vantage point I saw the man enter and recognized him as thief from the train. He was coatless with hairy chest showing behind his buttonless shirt, and he held his gun in his hand.

He gazed at me. "Well, looky here." He motioned with his pistol for the barber to move away. "This don't concern you, so stay out if it."

I couldn't see the barber but I heard him shuffle to the side of the room. I was glad for it because there was no reason for him to get hurt. The thief stepped to the front of the chair and looked down at me. "You don't look so tough now. I told you I would kill you, but I didn't think it would be this easy."

"Nothing easy about it, stranger. I suggest you think twice about what you're about to do."

He grimaced at the pain in his lip as his face broke into an evil grin. "Don't need to do no thinking. It's like fish in a barrel. You crossed me and you'll pay." He cocked his gun and brought it up.

The gunshot was loud in the room and smoke rose from the bullet hole in the cloth on my lap. The man looked at me stupidly with uncomprehending eyes, then he looked down at the tiny hole over his heart.

I clucked my tongue. "You should always make it a point to see what the fish is holding in his hand."

The man fell backwards, crashing into the table and chair where the barber had been reading the newspaper when I came in. I leaned up slightly to see him there, then turned to the barber. He looked at me with surprise and wonderment.

"How... ?"

I lifted the cloth to show the .45 in my hand. "When a man threatens to kill you, you should always be ready. I didn't know if he'd find me here or not, but I knew if he did I wouldn't be able to draw, so I held my gun on my lap." I leaned back into the chair. "If you'll find the local sheriff to let him know what happened, I'll just wait here until you can finish my shave."

He glanced to the dead man then back to me. "Yes, sir." He left in a hurry.

I pressed my finger through the hole in the cloth and watched it wiggle, glad the hole was from the inside out rather than from the outside in.

Chapter 2

I sat up as the local sheriff, followed by the barber, rushed into the room. He bent to the dead man, then straightened and stepped closer to me.

"You killed him?"

"I did."

"Why?"

I glanced to the barber, wondering why he hadn't told the story, then it dawned on me that the sheriff hadn't waited to be told anything. I looked back to the lawman. "He had a gun on me and was getting ready to shoot. I shot in self-defense." I nodded to the barber. "Ask him."

He turned. "Okay, Abe, tell me what

happened."

"It was just like he says. The man came in with gun drawn and orders me out of the way, then says something about fish in a barrel. Next thing I know he cocks his pistol and gets ready to shoot." He slowly brought his pointing finger up in reenactment. "I was sure he'd shot and killed this man," he pointed at me, "but the shot came from under the cloth. It was self-defense all right, I'll swear to it."

I leaned forward as the sheriff turned to me. The cloth fell from my chest and his eyes were drawn to the badge. "You're a U.S. Marshal?"

"Yes, sir." I brought my hand from under the cloth. "Branson Hawk. Pleased to meet you."

He shook my hand then glanced to the dead man. "Any reason why he'd want to kill you?"

I nodded. "Had a little run in on the train from Santa Fe. He stole a young lady's handbag. I got it back and he didn't like it."

He rubbed his chin with his fingers. "I see. Had you ever seen him before?

I shook my head.

He turned toward the barber then back to me. "Do you know his name?"

"No, sir."

"Then there is nothing left for me to do here." He stepped back. "Abe, I'll have the doc come get him, whoever he is, and get him ready for burial." With that, the sheriff left with a shake of his head.

I leaned back in the chair and spread the cloth over my torso. "Abe, if you don't mind I'd like to get on with my shave."

When finished, I ate a leisurely meal at the restaurant in the lobby of the hotel. I sat close to the door in hopes Miss Trudeau would come and we could eat together. Typically I was uncomfortable around women, but after meeting her and spending a short while together on the train, I felt extraordinarily brave. While waiting for her, I brushed the lint from my coat and fiddled with my string tie, but it was in vain because she never arrived. I grew self-conscious at sitting alone so long at the table with my meal finished, so at length and utterly disappointed, I rose, then climbed the stairs to my room and blew out the lamp.

I've always been able to go to sleep as soon as my head hit the pillow and that night was no exception. I drifted off with thoughts of her beautiful face and hoped for another pleasant train ride with her at my side.

After a good night's sleep in a soft bed, I washed my face and combed my hair with my fingers, then exited my room just in time to see her dragging her case down the stairs.

She looked up as I hurried to take it. "Thank you Mr. Hawk, but I can manage." She was shockingly cold and unfriendly.

Her demeanor surprised me for I thought we'd parted on good terms the day before. I looked at her and shook my head. "No ma'am. I can carry it and we can go to the depot together."

She removed her hand, stepped back and eyed me with an expression of disgust. "I must insist, sir, that you go along without me. In Santa Fe, the men are civilized. There is no murder in the shops of the city. You helped me on the train and for that I am thankful, but I have no intention of riding to Benson next to a killer."

I stood to look her in the eye, wondering how

she'd heard of the events in the barbershop. I had no remorse for the killing and I had no intention of denying that I'd done it. The thief had faced a stacked deck and had pushed me even though I'd tried to warn him.

Miss Trudeau stared back at me with an unattractive frown. I shook my head then jerked the case from the floor and stomped down the stairs. I didn't stop to wait for her but pushed on to the street toward the depot. She could walk with me or not, but no matter what she thought of me, I would carry her bag all the way.

I placed the bag in front of the ticket window so she could arrange for it to be loaded on the baggage car. As for me, I'd take the last seat on the last car and that would be that. By that time she stood only ten feet away. I nodded to her, my duty done. If she didn't want anything to do with me then so be it. I would act the gentleman no matter what.

She swallowed. "Thank you."

I nodded then turned toward the tracks to step aboard the last car and make my way to the very back seat. When I sat, I could see my fellow passengers. There were businessmen, cowboys and a few ladies in colorful dresses and tall hats. I sat with a frown and folded my arms, upset that she'd treated me like a murderer, and more upset that I'd let it bother me.

The whistle blew at the appointed time and I was happy when the car jerked into motion and we were off. The sooner I could get to Benson and on to Tucson, the sooner I'd get my next assignment from the Colonel.

As the sun traipsed higher in the sky, the desert morning cold gave way to comfortable,

Arizona winter pleasantness. At the start of the trip, the constant flow of air blowing into and through the cars had been cold and uncomfortable, but the nearness of the noon hour had brought the warmth I had grown accustomed to since arriving in Tucson from Kansas some fifteen years before. The train stopped in Bowie for water so I disembarked and took a stroll alongside the tracks to stretch my legs. In contrast to my car, the forward cars were surprisingly full of passengers that day. I stood in the sun with my thumbs poked into the pockets of my jeans and watched as riders swarmed like ants to the barren land next to the tracks.

I caught sight of a smallish woman in black as she stepped down the steps and onto the dirt. I recognized her immediately as Miss Trudeau and my heart leapt in my chest. I shook my head. What was I thinking? She had made it clear she wanted no part of my company. She turned and our eyes met. She dropped her head for an instant then looked at me again. Our eyes locked and I was lost. With a nervous swallow, I came to realize how much I wanted to sit next to her and continue our pleasant conversation of the day before.

I strolled to her side, happy that she remained where she stood and allowed me to approach. I nodded, but as so often was the case in my interactions with women, I could think of nothing to say.

She stared at me, waiting while shifting from foot to foot. The uncomfortable silence grew unbearable and I felt the fool. I could face a man in a gun battle, but I couldn't so much as say hello to a woman.

Finally, she tilted her head and favored me

with a half-smile.

My relief was immediate and my tongue suddenly came to life. "Miss Trudeau, I've felt some ashamed that you think so poorly of me. I was hoping we could talk about it. Perhaps if you heard my side of the story, you would understand why I did what I did."

She frowned and raised her palms in a shrug. "Mr. Hawk, I'd like to apologize. The hotel clerk told me last night that you'd killed a man. I was appalled that death could come so easily to your hand." She looked away for a moment, then gazed at me. "Then on the train I heard a man telling his seatmate about the incident, what you did and why." She rubbed her small bag with her thumbs. "I jumped to an incorrect conclusion. I've misjudged you and I'm sorry."

Her apology was music to my ears and I must confess that her change in attitude brought a contented smile to my face. I'd hoped all along that when she learned the truth, she would see I had done what was needed.

The conductor walked along the siding. "Two minutes. Two more minutes."

Passengers climbed the steps into the cars and I looked to the last car, anxious to board. I had no intention of getting left in the middle of nowhere. I tilted my head, unsure of exactly what to do. She had apologized, but that seemed to be the end of it. She hadn't stepped closer and hadn't given me any indication that she wished to continue our conversation, although I certainly did. I turned to her. "Thank you for the apology. I'm so glad we've come to an understanding." I shifted to see the other passengers boarding. "The train will be leaving soon.

We'd best be climbing on if we want to continue our trip." I nodded then pointed toward the end car. "I so enjoyed our time yesterday, perhaps you would consider riding with me the rest of the way to Benson?"

Her eyes darted left and right and it was easy for me to see that she was uncomfortable with the suggestion. Her recovery was rapid, she stepped close, the uncomfortable expression gone from her face as quickly as it had appeared. When she looked at me, her eyes opened wide and I stared, mesmerized, into the lovely pools of ocean blue.

My whole soul wanted to invite her again, but she had conveyed her message with exactness. I waved my hand. "Never mind. You go on to your seat and I'll go to mine."

She nodded and turned tentatively, then casting a glance my direction, she hurried to the cars at the front of the train where people were boarding. I watched briefly, then with a frown, stomped to the last car and climbed the iron steps.

I tried to sleep in the rocking car but had no luck. All I could think about was Miss Trudeau. I was certain that if we could spend more time together, we would become friends, but she had made her choice and there was nothing I could do about that. Eventually the train slowed and as the station platform came into view, the sign tacked to the side of the building read BENSON. I could see the escaping steam filling the station and the train staggered slightly, jerked forward then instantly back before coming to a complete stop.

I looked at the station and thought again of Miss Trudeau. She was grieving and scared in a strange town with no friends or acquaintances. I felt sorry for her and wondered about my trip. On my part, a small delay in returning to Tucson would be inconsequential. I could stay with her and offer my assistance. After all, isn't that what a concerned lawman should do? I stood from my seat and stuffed my thumbs into my pockets with a scowl. That would be a fine plan except for one thing, she didn't want me anywhere around.

I stepped from the train and immediately stretched my neck to find her. I saw her leaning from the car while peering from side to side as though she was looking for someone, but I knew she was coming alone. Alone! That clinched it. I would help even if she didn't want me to.

I tucked my satchel under may arm and threaded my way through disembarking passengers to where she stood. "Perhaps you'd like me to accompany you?"

Her eyes darted nervously under the veil before she quickly looked away. "I can't ask you to do that." She waved her arm at the train. "I'm sure you are anxious to take care of your business and return to Tucson. I can't ask you to do more."

I stood taller, proud of myself for being the kind of lawman who cared about the innocent and defenseless. "Nonsense. I'll stay with you until you no longer need me."

She took a deep breath. "I'm sure you are far too busy." She opened and closed her gloved hands.

I stood and held my hand for her. "I'm staying with you and that's all there is to it."

She tentatively took my hand and stepped to the dirt at the side of the train because the small platform at the Benson station was only large enough for the freight.

"You are here for your brother. Do you know where you are supposed to go?"

She shook her head and reached into her handbag for a yellow telegraph paper, which she held to me.

"If it's all the same to you I'd rather go first to the hotel before going to the mine to see about my brother." She pointed to the paper.

I unfolded the message. "This says you are supposed to meet with George Marks at the smelter?"

She nodded. "That's right."

I handed the paper back and pointed to a tall smokestack on a hill roughly a mile south and west of the train station. "It's over there. I'll take you now."

She turned to see the structure and the heavy, black smoke pouring from the top. She wrinkled her nose. "Is that the mine?"

"Actually, it is not a mine, it's called a smelter. The mines in the area, Tombstone to the south, Johnson to the east and others to the north, ship their ore to Benson to have it melted and separated so it can be sold." I waved toward the stack. "They refine silver and gold here."

She nodded, content with my rudimentary explanation. Truth be told, that's about all I knew of smelting so I was happy she hadn't asked any more questions.

I tucked her arm into mine and pointed to the rapidly expanding town. "Shall we find a means of transportation to take us there?"

"But my bag?"

I waved offhandedly. "Your bag will be here when we return. I've always found it best to take care of the unpleasant task first. Postponing won't make it any easier."

We arrived at smelter hill in a six-mule-team freight wagon after offering the teamster two dollars to drive us there. As the driver pulled to a stop in front of a low, red brick building, I jumped to the ground and lifted her to stand next to me. The driver pocketed the bills with a tooth-filled grin, then with unrestrained cursing, bade the hapless animals back toward town. She watched them go while shaking her head.

When the team and wagon were away, we entered the building. Several men with green eyeshades and rolled up sleeves worked at desks toward the front of the large room, while several men in business suits gathered in the back. One of the front men noticed us and stepped forward.

"Good afternoon."

We stepped closer. "We are here to meet with Mr. Marks."

He nodded and glanced to the back. "May I tell him who is inquiring?"

She spoke for the first time. "I'm Trudy Trudeau."

"One moment please." He nodded and hurried to the back.

We saw the clerk walk to a tall man with broad shoulders who'd been speaking animatedly to the others. Both men turned toward us and the clerk pointed our direction. Marks turned, said something to the men in the group, then strode toward us with long, purposeful strides.

He took Miss Trudeau's hand and kissed it lightly. "Thank you for coming." He waved his arm toward the back. "We are all sorry for your loss."

She swallowed hard. "Thank you."
He turned to me. "Is this your husband?"

Chapter 3

I coughed at a sudden catch in my throat and the most uncomfortable coldness raced from my back to my chest. I'd never been accused of being married and the implication struck me hard.

Before I could answer, she shook her head and quickly removed her hand from my arm. "No. May I present Branson Hawk, U.S. Marshal."

Marks shook my hand with a quizzical expression. "Is there a reason for the U.S. Marshals to be involved? The death was accidental."

I slowly shook my head. "I am not on assignment. I was fortunate enough to meet Miss Trudeau on the train. When she told me her plight, I offered to escort her to retrieve her brother."

He breathed, seemingly relieved that my appearance was the result of a chance meeting rather than an official visit. The reaction was not uncommon and I couldn't blame him. There was a dead man and I was a U.S. Marshal.

"I see." He frowned as he turned his attention to her. "The company has made all the arrangements for you to accompany your brother back home. He is in the ingot room and will remain there until the next eastbound train. Your ticket home as well as his freight charge has been paid, and if there is anything more the company can do, please let me know."

She lifted the veil enough to wipe her eyes. "Thank you." She sobbed and was suddenly weak. She reached for my arm for support and I held her until she regained her composure. She wiped her eyes again.

I placed an arm around her waist before turning to Mr. Marks. "I suppose we should have her identify the body."

She stiffened in my arms. I knew it would be a disagreeable task but one that needed done.

Marks frowned and gazed at her. "I'm not sure that is in your best interest, ma'am. Peter was at the furnace when he was struck in the head by a swinging set of oversized pulleys that had broken loose from the wall." He swallowed. "It's not a pretty sight."

She shuddered and gripped more tightly to my arm. "I'm sure there is no reason to see him."

I cocked my head. "I'm afraid it is customary. I've known of instances where the dead man was incorrectly identified. As a lawman, I suggest you make sure."

She swallowed hard and took a deep breath.

"Very well."

The smelter manager shook his head. "Of course. If you'd care to wait here for a few minutes, I'll make the arrangements." He pointed to a chair then left to talk with the man who'd first welcomed us.

Miss Trudeau sat ramrod straight in a hard, wooden chair while I waited at her side. Marks soon returned with another man following. He nodded at me then turned to the lady.

"The ingot room is a quarter mile from here. I've sent instructions to bring my personal carriage around the front and I've asked Mr. Livingston to escort you." He gestured toward the new man. "He's in charge of bookkeeping where your brother worked."

Miss Trudeau stood and shook the hands of both men. "Thank you so much for your kindness."

Marks bowed slightly then backed away, leaving three of us standing close to the door while waiting for the carriage. The new man shifted nervously from foot to foot and fidgeted with his bowler hat in his hands. He kept studying me, glancing from my face to the badge on my chest and back. I got the impression he wanted to tell me something, but was hesitant.

Less than two minutes later the door opened and a worker stepped through. He nodded to Livingston. "I've brought the carriage around, sir." He held the door open. "If y'all will step this way I'll drive you to the ingot room."

We climbed into the canvas-topped carriage, Miss Trudeau and I in the back and the driver and Livingston in the front. The driver slapped the reins on the matched team of bays and the light carriage jolted forward. We rode in silence toward the huge smokestack. As we got closer, we passed through a wide, flat area with what looked like thousands of stacks of wood.

Livingston waved his arm. "We buy hundreds of cords of wood from the locals. For the first time in many of their lives they have money they need to buy necessities."

As he said it, I noticed a swarthy, sombrero-wearing Mexican man with a colorful serape over his shoulders leading a donkey with sticks piled high. They were followed by a barefoot youngster who looked at us with wide eyes. They stopped to watch us pass by.

Livingston touched the driver's arm. "Hold up for a minute." He then waved for the boy to come to the carriage.

The father waited, looking over the back of the donkey while the son, grinning widely, stood next to the front wheel of our carriage. Livingston reached into a vest pocket and pulled out a small candy. He brushed the lint away then passed it down to the excited youngster.

"For you, Juan."

The boy wasted no time in plopping the candy into his mouth and shifting it to one side of his jaw. "Thank you, señor." He turned and ran to his father who waved toward Livingston with a nod of appreciation before turning and trudging ahead on the hard-packed dirt.

Livingston motioned for the driver to continue, then he turned to Miss Trudeau and me as the carriage jerked forward. "Juan lives with his family in a little adobe shack directly behind the ingot room." He pointed ahead. "Before the smelter came they barely survived with a handful of chickens, a goat and a donkey. I first met him when his father sent him to tell me that three men had come in the night to knock the wall down. Carlos, that's the father, chased them away and has become the unofficial guard at the back of the property. He won't accept any money other than what we pay for the wood he delivers, but every time I see them, I give Juan a piece of candy, and that seems to make them happy." He smiled smugly then turned back to the front.

Silence again in the carriage, the only sound the soft clip-clop of the horses on the hard packed dirt as they trotted along. Miss Trudeau leaned forward and tapped Mr. Livingston on the shoulder.

"What is an ingot room?"

He glanced quickly at me then returned his attention to her. "When the ore is refined, we pour either silver or gold into molds. When the metal cools and hardens, it's called an ingot. The ingot room is where we store those until they are shipped out to the buyers."

She nodded, satisfied at the explanation, then leaned back and folded her arms.

The horses clip-clopped along on the hard packed road and there was no further conversation. I looked into the distances of the pleasant little valley. In the cloudless, winter day, I could see tall cottonwoods marking the meandering path of the San Pedro River to the southeast. I glanced left and right, then concentrated on the structures to our front. I'd only seen the smokestack from afar and as we closed the distance, I was surprised that it was even taller than I had supposed. Two long, low buildings on either side were attached to the base and workers could be seen coming in and out of the one to the east. Lined up on a road extending into the expanse, teamsters directing ten-horse-teams drove oversized ore wagons through huge doors. Our driver turned west, past an identical, windowless, apparently unoccupied but connected building on the other side. He pulled to a stop on a dusty path in front of a large door, then jumped down to assist Miss Trudeau. He stayed with the carriage while Livingston escorted her and me to a huge swinging door. He pulled a set of keys from his vest and unlocked a large padlock, then pulled the chain through oversized metal rings on the door. The heavy chain plopped to the ground with a deep rattle and Livingston pushed the thick, wooden door open only enough for a person to squeeze through.

We stepped inside. The huge room was cave-like, dark and surprisingly chilly given the proximity to the blast furnace only fifty yards away. I looked at the brick structure that made the base of the smokestack, which rose through the ceiling and beyond. Several holes had been cut into the roof on the west side of the building and with the aid of the light coming in, I could see scores of workers scurrying from place to place. Many had shovels to unload the ore wagons, pushing the crushed rocks into a bin at the side, while others stoked the firebox by expertly throwing arm-sized sticks into the flames through a square opening.

Livingston took a lantern from a post and lit it with a match from his pocket. When he slid the globe down, the eerie light penetrated the darkness only enough to see a few feet ahead. He led the way across the cavernous room and stopped at what appeared to be a tarp-covered bench. He stepped closer then pushed the lantern into my hand and pulled the tarp, letting it slide to the ground on the side. I held the light higher and stepped forward, still holding one of Miss Trudeau's arms, and immediately recognized a coffin placed on large blocks of ice. Livingston slid the coffin lid until he could pick it up and place it to the side, then he stepped back to allow Miss Trudeau access.

At the sight of her dead brother, she wailed and fell across the casket, sobbing with great gasps. Livingston and I looked away, allowing a grieving sister a moment alone with her dead brother. I clumsily held lightly to her arm and involuntarily shivered.

After what I'd assumed was an appropriate amount of time because her shrieks had diminished, I tugged lightly on Miss Trudeau's arm. She pushed herself up from the open casket then wrapped her arms tightly around my neck. She buried her head in my shoulder and I held her there for a long time. Finally, she pushed away and wiped her eyes and nose with her kerchief, then stared up at me.

"I'm sorry Mr. Hawk. Please forgive me."

"Don't you worry your pretty little head. I'm happy to be here."

She turned back to the casket, bravely forcing control and holding her tears. She rubbed the wood then stepped away.

I glanced for the first time at the man in the box. To call him a big man was an understatement. Huge, meaty hands rested, one on the other, over a massive chest, and one of his legs seemed as thick as my waist. I gazed at his head, remembering the explanation that he'd been hit by a swinging set of pulleys. They'd done tremendous damage and I cringed at the sight.

I looked to Miss Trudeau. She chewed her bottom lip then glanced toward the door. I took that as a sign that she was ready to leave. I held the lamp high as Livingston replaced the lid and the tarp, then we walked three abreast to the door.

The sun seemed extra bright as we exited and the afternoon warmth felt good on my shoulders. I squinted as I took the woman's arm and assisted her into the carriage. I started to climb in, but Livingston, who continued to stand at the door, caught my attention. With a small movement of his head, he beckoned me.

"Excuse me Miss Trudeau. I'll be right back." I walked to the man's side. "Yes, sir?"

He swallowed, then pointed to my badge with his nose. "Are you here on official business?"

I thought it odd that both he and Marks were so concerned about my visit, but then, it wasn't uncommon for folks to think they might be in trouble, and with a dead man, even an accidentally dead man, I could understand their concern.

I looked toward Miss Trudeau in the carriage then leaned close to Livingston's ear. "No. I met Miss Trudeau on the train and offered my assistance, that's all."

He seemed disappointed. He frowned and scraped at the dust next to the door with his boot toe. "I see." One of the horses stamped and Livingston glanced up. "Then I suppose we should go." He turned and locked the padlock around the chain.

I waited. Something was bothering the man and my curiosity was building. My instincts told me he wanted to tell me something but he needed some encouragement. I touched the sleeve of his coat. "Is something bothering you?"

He quickly looked up, eyes wide. "No."

His answer was too hurried. He did have something to tell me, and there was something else. He was afraid.

Chapter 4

Livingston stepped immediately toward the carriage and although I wanted to stop him, I let him go and followed behind. He climbed into the front seat and kept his eyes forward in an obvious maneuver to keep from looking at me or Miss Trudeau. After I'd climbed to sit next to her, the driver turned the horses back toward the main office building and urged them into a trot.

Miss Trudeau sat with head down and hands folded on her lap. Her gloved fingers fidgeted, but the rest of her body was still except for the slight movement of her shallow breathing. There was no conversation from any of the four of us.

We passed by the Mexican man and his son

now leading the unburdened burro out of firewood enclosure. As before, they stopped and waved and watched us pass by, then in only a few minutes we encountered two more serape wearing men leading small burrows laden with wood. The driver nodded to them and they smiled and waved cheerily.

The matching set of bays dropped their heads in quiet resolution when the driver pulled them to a stop in front of the office building. Livingston climbed down then turned and removed his hat.

"Miss Trudeau." He pointed to the driver. "Shorty here will take you to the hotel. The company has paid the freight charge to take the casket back to Santa Fe on the next eastbound train. That will be Thursday and we'll make sure to get your brother to the freight car in plenty of time. You'll have a couple of days of waiting, not much we can do about that, but in the meantime, we'll keep the ice changed out to keep the body cool."

She nodded bravely then dropped her head to continue studying her fidgeting hands. I looked at Livingston and he nervously returned my gaze for only the briefest of moments before turning his attention to the driver.

"Shorty, take these folks wherever they need to go."

Shorty nodded then turned in the seat. "Where to, sir?"

I waited for Miss Trudeau but she made no effort to look up. I knew her bag was at the station and there was only one hotel in town that was nice enough to suit the needs of such a fine lady. I pointed toward town. "To the train station for her bag then to the Occidental Hotel."

As the carriage turned and started away, I

glanced over my shoulder. From my seat next to Miss Trudeau, I watched as Livingston stood with his hat in his hand, his spectacles reflecting the sun's bright light. I nodded but he made no return gesture. Finally, he turned and walked back into the building.

The train station was practically deserted when we arrived. Miss Trudeau hadn't spoken since the smelter and when the carriage pulled to a stop, she continued to sit, seemingly oblivious to her surroundings. I stepped from the carriage and skipped up the steps to the platform and into the door of the baggage repository. An old, white-haired gentleman with a clipboard in hand turned when he heard my boots on the rough-cut boards.

"Afternoon, young feller."

I glanced around the room, seeing travel trunks and barrels and packages stacked neatly at each wall. "Howdy. I've come to pick up a bag for Miss Trudeau. It was on the train from Deming today."

He scrolled down the paperwork on the clipboard then looked up with a narrow grin. "Yes, sir." He walked to the west wall and pulled the bag from a knee-high shelf.

I recognized it as the same bag I'd carried to the Deming station that morning so I reached and hefted it. "Thank you, friend."

His grin expanded. "My pleasure. You have a wonderful day."

I smiled at his pleasantries. "I'll do that, and the same to you."

I lifted the bag onto the floorboard of the buggy, then climbed to take my seat next to Miss Trudeau. She didn't speak so I nodded permission for Shorty to head to the hotel. He clucked to the bays. They pushed into their collars and we headed to the business street of the growing town.

Benson was alive in the early afternoon sunlight. People milled about, in and out of the shops, and of course, each of the saloons seemed to be doing a rousing business even though it was far from dark. The Occidental Hotel was the largest building on the street, and in contrast to many of the older buildings, it was freshly whitewashed. When the carriage came to rest, I jumped down and walked around to help her to the street.

She stepped gracefully to the dirt by using my arm to steady herself. As she stood at my side, I glanced to Shorty. "I'll be back to get the bag in a moment."

I waited for a nod of understanding, then I took her hand and placed it on my elbow and we climbed the steps to the boardwalk. She hesitated, then placed her other hand on my arm.

"Thank you again, Mr. Hawk. I don't know what I'd have done if you weren't here to help."

I patted her hand then held the hotel door for her to enter the opulent lobby. We strolled to the counter where a tall, thin man in a white shirt and lacy black armbands waited. I left her there to register and walked back outside to retrieve her bag and to talk to Shorty.

He grinned good-naturedly as I stepped close. "If there's nothing else I'll be heading back to the offices."

I leaned against the carriage. "Would you be willing to wait for another couple of minutes? I'd like to ride back out with you."

He shrugged. "Fine by me."

I nodded then lifted the bag. "I'll be right back."

By the time I got to the desk, Miss Trudeau had signed the book and was waiting patiently at the stairs with a uniformed man. She peered at me forlornly as I approached and he reached for the bag. I handed it over and watched as she climbed the steps with the porter following three steps behind. She paused at the landing and leaned on the railing as she looked down.

"Thank you again, Mr. Hawk. I'm sorry to have caused you a delay. Now that you have done your duty, I'll release you. You may continue your business and proceed to Tucson."

I swallowed, suddenly uncomfortable. I'd always been awkward around beautiful women but my interaction with Miss Trudeau was bringing out the best in me, and it was an association I was enjoying, although there had been no indication that the friendship might progress. I cleared my throat. "I will be in town until at least tomorrow. Perhaps we could eat together this evening?"

As I looked at her, I thought I saw a reserved, almost non-existent smile. What could anyone expect after the ordeal of seeing her dead brother? But it seemed to me to be a smile nonetheless and it brightened the entire room.

"Perhaps another time. I'm much too distraught."

I stood on the lobby floor looking up at her. "I won't take no for an answer. At times like these, it is best not to be alone. I'll meet you for supper."

She nodded with a sigh, then turned to shuffle down the hall to her room.

With a spring in my step, I strolled to the

waiting carriage and climbed in. Shorty's grin as I sat next to him in the front seat embarrassed me. I shook my head. I was acting like a half-grown pup and I had to look away to keep him from seeing my expression. He chuckled to himself then clucked to the horses. They leaned into their harnesses and made a wide turn in the middle of the street. In minutes we were out of town, advancing along the road to the smelter.

I looked at the tall stack as we approached and wondered at the odd behavior of Mr. Livingston. In truth, that was the reason I'd decided to return. I'd seen the look on his face and felt like he desperately wanted to tell me something, but was afraid. It was lawman's instinct, I supposed, but that instinct had served me well and I tried to always honor the feelings when they came.

I appreciated Shorty's quiet companionship. He drove the team and we covered the ground as he hummed a tune, unconcerned about my presence or my business. It was as if he was refreshed at the opportunity to be with someone without the obligation to converse. I smiled at the thought for that was exactly my preference. When he pulled the team to a stop, I jumped down and reached to shake his hand.

"Thank you, Shorty. I appreciate you driving me back out here."

He shrugged again then smiled and slapped the reins to the matched team.

I turned directly to the same entrance door we'd passed through earlier in the day. As before, the front office clerks bent over their desks in unhurried diligence, but the closest looked up, then stood and approached.

"May I help you?"

I glanced over his shoulder in a fast search for Livingston, but didn't see him. I looked at the young man. "I'd like to speak with Mr. Livingston if it wouldn't be too much trouble."

The man nodded. "Of course. Right this way."

He motioned to the left and led the way with me striding to keep up. We passed through a door into another large room with several identically dressed clerks bent over their desks. We stopped at one of the desks and an even younger clerk peered at us over the top of his horn-rimmed glasses.

"Yes?"

"Man to see Mr. Livingston."

The new clerk stood and bade me follow him toward the back through a maze of desks and workers. Finally, I saw Livingston standing at an open door gazing toward the stack and low buildings we'd been in only two hours earlier. He turned as though he felt my eyes. When he saw me, his face grew immediately pale and he cautiously glanced from side to side. Shortly, he shook his head then strode to meet me.

He smiled weakly, extended his hand and spoke with exaggerated confidence. "Mr. Hawk. What brings you back?"

"Good afternoon, Mr. Livingston. I wondered if I might have a word with you?" I glanced at the clerk who continued to stand nearby. "In private."

Livingston swallowed then nodded to the clerk. "Thanks, Johnny. You can go back to work now."

"Yes, sir." Johnny turned and marched back to his desk.

Livingston pointed toward the open door with

his nose. "Would you like to step outside?"

"Yes, that would be ideal."

He motioned for me to go first and he followed me to the outside. I stopped to gaze at the tall stack and could see a well-worn path from this door through the brush next to the wood yard, eventually leading to the big door of the ingot room where the coffin rested on ice under a tarp.

He stepped to my side, took off his glasses and cleaned them with a cloth he'd pulled from his pocket. "What did you want to see me about, Mr. Hawk?"

I tried to smile for I didn't want him to feel threatened, but the forced attempt had the opposite effect. He grew increasingly nervous and rubbed all the harder on the spectacles.

I wiped the smile off my face then turned to the man and tapped my badge. "Mr. Livingston, I'm a Deputy U.S. Marshal, but as I told you earlier, I'm not here for any official reason other than to assist the woman you met earlier." I paused, letting what I'd said register.

He seemed to calm slightly so I continued, pointing toward the low building. "You took us to what you called the ingot room, but while there you seemed preoccupied. I got the distinct impression there was something you wanted to tell me. I decided to come back and give you that opportunity."

He took a deep breath while reaching behind me to close the door to the office building. From there he motioned ahead with his nose, then took another five steps into the brush. I followed.

He replaced the cleaning cloth to his pocket and pulled his glasses over his ears, then nervously rubbed his hands as he looked at me. "I seem to be missing a gold ingot." He pointed toward the room. "We are very diligent in keeping our inventories accurate, but only last week we, Peter and I, discovered the discrepancy." Livingston scratched the dirt with his boot. "Mr. Marks doesn't know. I've been hoping to find it before he learns it's gone, but if we don't find it soon, I'll be fired."

I frowned at his exceeding concern over a few ounces of gold. Surely the threat of being fired was not as likely as he supposed. I glanced at the deep footpath leading to the room. Any of the workers could have secretly slipped one or more ingots into their pockets and no one would have been aware.

I hitched my pants to my hips. "Mr. Livingston, don't you think you are overly concerned at the loss of a small amount of gold?"

His eyes grew wide. "I don't think you understand. An ingot weighs nearly three hundred pounds and it's almost pure gold. No one just walks off with that stuffed under their shirt."

My jaw dropped and my brain quickly ran the numbers. Three hundred pounds of gold was something under five thousand ounces. I swallowed and shook my head. "That's over a hundred thousand dollars."

His lips pressed together. "More like eighty thousand with the impurities, but that's still a lot of money." He pulled the set of keys from his vest and dangled them in front of my face. "There are only two keys to the lock on the door. I have one," he rattled the keys, "and Mr. Marks has one." He pointed toward the big door and the hard-packed road leading in and out. "Every wagon that enters that door is searched before it can leave the property so I'm convinced the gold is still somewhere in the building, but Peter and I looked high and low for it with no success." He shook his head and looked at me with fear-filled eyes. "Then Peter has an accident. It couldn't have come at a worse time. He was a good friend and at my request was searching for the ingot when it happened. He ordinarily would never have been in the smelter area. He was a bookkeeper and a good one, but he didn't know his way around there. I should never have asked him to go and I feel awful that he's dead." He clenched his jaw. "It's my fault."

My brain jumped from fact to fact as I tried to sort through the information. My first thought was of the dead man and the possibility that there had been no accident, that he'd been murdered if he was too close to finding the gold. I clucked my tongue. "Was it an accident?"

Livingston looked down and rubbed his face with his hands before returning his gaze to me. "I thought at first of the possibility that he'd been killed because of the missing gold, but I've investigated thoroughly. At least three of the fire tenders on that side of the building indicated there was no one else anywhere close to the pulleys when they broke loose. Peter was unfortunately in the wrong place at the wrong time."

I grunted my skepticism.

He shook his head again. "I know it seems there is a connection, and for a couple of days I was convinced there was, but think about it, other than the thief, no one but Peter and I knew the ingot was missing, no one but me knew he was searching for it, so no one would have had a reason to hurt him." His eyes squinted as he frowned. "And just in case you think I had any part of it, I can tell you with absolute surety that I did not kill him. The only logical explanation is an unfortunate accident."

I pursed my lips, not completely agreeing with his logic because there were too many unanswered questions about the death and the circumstances. But there was more to the story than an accident or a murder. I shifted my thoughts to the missing gold. Three hundred pounds! A fortune!

Possibilities raced and I deposited different facts in different corners of my mind. Every new thought seemed to bounce around, nudging against the facts, curling in and out and around them and coming away either stronger or weaker because of it. It's the only way I can describe how my mind works when dissecting the information about a case, and this was suddenly a case I was bound and determined to solve.

Chapter 5

A small gust of wind flapped the tails of my coat bringing me out of my thoughts. Livingston nervously cocked his head as he stared at me. He chewed on a fingernail then glanced toward the closed door at our backs.

He leaned close. "What do you suggest?"

I turned to gaze at the smokestack and wondered at the coincidence of missing gold worth close to a hundred thousand dollars and a dead man. There had to be a connection and I felt a deep, seething anger that Miss Trudeau was now without a brother and had the unpleasant task of taking the body back to Santa Fe for burial. I wanted to find the missing gold for Livingston, but more than that, I wanted to solve the case of the death of Peter Trudeau for her.

I turned back to Livingston. "Are you requesting my help?"

With lips pursed, he nodded without speaking.

I glanced toward the main office building. "Do you trust Mr. Marks?"

His eyebrows pulled down. "Mr. Marks?"

"Yes. You said the two of you are the only ones with keys to the ingot room." I waved my arm in a wide arc. "And he's the head man of the entire facility, is he not?"

"He is."

"Is there any possible way he might be involved in the theft of the gold?"

Livingston's eyes opened wide. "Absolutely not! He is a trusted man. A man well thought of by all who know him. I'd never believe he had anything to do with the disappearance of the ingot."

I nodded. "Then the first thing to do is to inform him of the missing gold and make sure he agrees to allow me to start investigating."

Livingston's face fell in a stricken expression and his shoulders slumped as he exhaled. "I'll get fired."

"That is a possibility, but I think not. You are sure the ingot has not left the building. If that is the case, it is not gone but temporarily missing."

He glanced up, a glimmer of hope showing in his eyes. "I'm quite positive the ingot remains somewhere within the smelter structures."

I pointed toward the office building with my nose. "I suggest we tell him now."

Livingston bravely nodded then stepped and opened the door. Together we walked through the maze of desks until we reached a private office on the other side of the office building. He gently rapped on the door.

"Come in."

Marks glanced at Livingston then studied me as we walked in. I was sure he wondered why I'd returned.

He stepped around the desk and held his hand for a shake. "Good afternoon Mr. ...uh?"

"Hawk. Branson Hawk."

"Yes, of course. Sorry. How can we be of assistance?"

I shook my head. "The question is how I can be of assistance to you."

He turned to Livingston with a questioning expression then returned his gaze to me. "I don't understand."

Livingston stepped forward. "There is something you need to know."

Marks frowned and motioned for us to take seats while he took his own at the desk. Behind him a set of windows showed the large buildings under the smokestack although from our vantage point we couldn't see the smoke from the top. Marks sat and clasped his hands over his abundant stomach while leaning back against the seat. He looked toward us expectantly.

Livingston cleared his throat and licked his lips. "I'm afraid a gold ingot is missing."

Marks bolted forward in his chair and slammed his palms on the desk. His eyes widened and he had trouble catching his breath. "Missing?"

"Yes, sir." Livingston glanced quickly at me before continuing. "I'm sure it is still on the property, but it is gone from the ingot room."

Marks rubbed his hands on the smooth reflection of the mahogany desk and looked down as he forced himself to take a centering breath. At length his head came up and he turned his attention to me. "You said earlier that your visit was not official, but is this why you are here?"

I twirled my hat in my hands. "No, sir. As I said earlier, I chanced to meet Miss Trudeau on the train and offered my assistance. It was only when Livingston explained the missing ingot did my presence here become official. That is, of course, if you'd like me to become involved."

He nodded. "Yes. Absolutely. If you can help us find the ingot, we will all be appreciative." His eyes opened wide at a sudden thought. He turned to Livingston. "And Peter's death? Is there any connection?"

Livingston rung his hands. "I'm convinced Peter's death was an accident, but the Marshal here," he pointed to me, "seems to think there is a link."

Marks cocked his head. "Is that right, Marshal?"

I sat up in my chair. I hadn't done so much as an ounce of investigating, but my bones told me it had to be tied in somehow. "I believe so. The theft of that much gold, then the sudden death of the very man who is searching for it, is simply too much to be only a coincidence."

He nodded. "Then you should begin investigating right away. We will pledge our complete support. Anything you need, you just let Livingston know and he'll make sure to get it."

I nodded but realized I couldn't begin right away. It would be dark soon and I needed to telegraph Colonel Marcomb in Tucson to let him know the reason for my absence. I could only stay if he agreed, though I had no expectation that he'd say anything other than what he always said, "Hop to it, young man." I looked forward to getting started, but I smiled inwardly as I remembered the other reason I couldn't start my investigation immediately. I had an appointment with a beautiful woman for supper. I'd honor that agreement, then get a good night's sleep and be ready to start my investigation.

We got up to leave and I reached across the desk with an extended hand. "Unless Colonel Marcomb, the head of the Marshals in Tucson, refuses my request to stay, I'll be back out in the morning."

I caught a ride back to town in a wood-sided wagon taking workers back to Benson at the end of their shift. As the wagon lumbered past the telegraph office, I jumped out and stepped onto the boardwalk and through the door.

The operator stood as I entered. "Afternoon."

Unlike many telegraph offices I'd been in, the chest-high counter was bare except for a single pad and sharpened pencil placed neatly at the side. I leaned on my elbows. "Howdy back at you. I'd like to send a message."

He pointed to the pad then stepped away so I could write in privacy. I chuckled because he would be reading what I wrote in a matter of minutes, but it was a thoughtful gesture just the same. I took up the pencil, licked the tip, then wrote a quick message. He stepped forward when I ripped the paper from the pad and pushed it toward him. He took it and counted the words.

"Seventeen cents."

I reached into my pocket and counted the

change onto the counter, then slid the coins across. "If a return comes back this afternoon, I'd appreciate you sending it to the Occidental. If not, I'll stop back by in the morning."

He nodded, then sat and got comfortable while he lightly fingered the apparatus. I watched in admiration as he deftly clicked out the message. In less time than I'd expected, he turned to me with a nod and a smile. I touched the brim of my hat then turned to leave the small office. I stood for a moment under the veranda to watch the increasingly busy street. Horses lined the hitching rails in front of the saloons and two more wagons full of smelter workers creaked to a stop to allow the occupants to jump out, most quickly joining the cowboys in the drinking houses, and others shuffling down the side street to the residential part of town. I strolled directly to the hotel, where, at the invitation of the clerk, I signed the registration book. I ran my finger up the page until I reached the flowing script with the name Trudy Trudeau, and saw that she was in room six. The clerk reached into the cubbyholes behind his chair and pulled out my key to room eleven. I smiled as I took it and climbed the stairs.

I paused at room six, wondering if I should knock and let Miss Trudeau know that our plans for supper were unchanged, but decided against it. I'd go to my room and wash my face and hands to make myself presentable, then call on her.

Room eleven was bright and cheery because of the descending winter sun pouring through a large, west-facing window. I removed my coat and brushed the accumulated dust, then hung it carefully over the back of a chair. I removed my string tie then placed my shirt over the coat. I would have liked to have had a change of clothes, but I'd make do with what I had. I poured the water from a pitcher to a small basin atop a wooden shelf. The water was cold but it felt good on my face and neck. I combed my hair with my fingers then donned my shirt and took a moment to fix my tie just as I liked it.

I tucked my shirt into my pants then slipped into my coat. Pulling the lapels with a snap, I studied my reflection in the mirror, all the while thinking of the woman in room six. I sauntered there and knocked lightly. The door opened and I was gratified with the expression behind the mourning veil as she recognized me. I looked through the mesh at her blue eyes and blinked. She became more beautiful every time I saw her.

I bowed slightly and tipped my hat. "Dinner?" I stepped back so she could exit and lock the door, then I held my arm, which she grasped. Together we strolled to the landing, down the carpeted stairs and through the side door into the restaurant.

I held her chair as she sat, then I took my seat on the other side. She cocked her head and placed her elbows on the table and chin on her clasped hands.

I held her gaze as long as I could, then looked away, embarrassed at the scrutiny as her eyes locked on mine. I fidgeted with the cloth napkin on the table before gazing at her again. "If I were in your shoes, I doubt I would be half so composed."

She made no answer, but looked down at the white tablecloth to draw invisible circles with her gloved fingers. When the waiter appeared at our table, we ordered then sat quietly until the food arrived. We ate in silence. She wasn't in the mood for conversation and I honored that. She stared out the windows to the street and I stared at her, trying though probably not succeeding in keeping a hungry wolf expression from my face.

I ate everything on my plate, but she only picked and nibbled. I couldn't blame her. The sight of her dead brother in the casket must have been hard on her, and I was sure her thoughts were of him and the trip home.

I wiped my mouth with the napkin and cleared my throat. "I've asked permission to stay in Benson for a few days."

She turned to me with a frown. "Not on my account I hope."

I shook my head. "Not completely. There is a case I'll be working on, but I'll be around to help you with anything you need. Your train leaves day after tomorrow. I'll be there to get you situated."

She pushed her plate to the left and rubbed the cloth. "I can't ask you to do that."

"You didn't ask, but I'll be there. I've enjoyed our time together. It's the least I can do."

"But Mr. Hawk, I've intruded on your plans enough. Please don't stay on my account."

I waved my hand. "No use arguing. I said I would stay and I will."

She reached across the table with her hands facing up. I leaned forward and placed my hands in hers. She stared at me, then, in answer to my request, bravely smiled while squeezing my fingers.

Somehow I remembered a cold winter day in Kansas a lifetime earlier. I'd been about five-years-old and the wind through the house had chilled me to the bone. My mother sat on a chair and beckoned me sit on her lap. When I did, she wrapped a buffalo blanket around us and held me close. In some way, the warmth of Miss Trudeau's smile took me back to that long forgotten memory.

As I lay in my bed that night with fingers interlaced behind my head, I smiled. Miss Trudeau was a woman who seemed to bring out the best in me. With others, I'd always been awkward and came across as gruff or even mean. A cousin had tried to teach me to be gentler to the fairer sex, and I'd tried to change, but Miss Trudeau seemed to be the first girl who'd noticed. She hadn't seemed happy when I told her my trip to Tucson had been postponed for a few days, but I attributed that to her distress at seeing her dead and mangled brother. She had asked why, but I had been evasive because her brother was a part of the reason for my stay. I was sure she wanted to have the ordeal over and would not want to learn that I suspected murder. As for me, I was simply glad for the chance to see her as much as possible until her train left for Santa Fe.

We met again for a breakfast and chose the same table at the hotel restaurant. Her cheeks showed more color behind the veil and little by little it seemed the agony she felt at her brother's death was lessening. We talked of inconsequential things, each of us wishing to keep the thoughts of her brother out of the way. She had one more day of waiting and I didn't envy her, sitting hour after hour in the hotel room.

I leaned forward. "You should get out for some fresh air. It's not good that you stay cooped up all day in the hotel."

She looked out the windows to the busy street, then glanced down to the barely touched food on her plate. She shook her head. "There is nowhere I would like to go and nothing I would like to see. I'll be leaving tomorrow and will soon have this dreadful business finished." She sighed and wiped her eyes with the cloth napkin.

We said our goodbyes with a promise to meet again for supper, then I strolled to the telegraph office and stepped inside. The same operator stood when I entered, and at seeing me, he reached to the cubbyholes above the desk. He smiled as he found what he was looking for, then pushed the paper toward me. I unfolded it and read quickly. PERMISSION GRANTED TO INVESTIGATE MURDER AND THEFT IN BENSON.

I tapped the paper on my palm. I still didn't know for sure if Miss Trudeau's brother had actually been murdered, but that was what I'd investigate. I purposely hadn't included in my message to Tucson that the theft had been almost a hundred thousand dollars in gold because I didn't want that getting around the small town of Benson. I'd been impressed with this particular operator's attention to confidentiality, but that would have been big news, and with big news comes big temptation to spread it around. The more investigating I could do without every person in town knowing about it, the better it would be.

I hitched a ride on a freight wagon traveling south from town toward the smelter. I sat next to the ill-dressed, burley teamster with tobacco juice running down his chin and covering his shirt front. He cheerfully offered me a bite from his plug but I declined. He shrugged and replaced it to his shirt pocket then slapped the reins on the mules. I jumped out at the office buildings and stood for a moment, waving as the teamster grinned then spat a long, brown stream to the side before taking his load back to the buildings surrounding the smokestack.

The warmth from the rising, orange sun felt good on my back as I stepped to the office door. I paused before entering, looking through the glass to the clerks who occupied the desks this day. I entered and strolled inside, then waited patiently until one of the men saw me. He stood from his small writing platform.

"Good morning."

I stepped closer. "Good morning. I'm here to see Mr. Livingston."

He nodded and pointed to a hard-backed wooden chair against the wall. "If you'll wait there I'll go fetch him."

I glanced to a large clock on the wall and saw that it was already nine o'clock. I settled into the chair, crossed my legs and held my hat on my lap. Mr. Livingston and the clerk sauntered through the desks and Livingston walked directly to me and stepped for a handshake.

"Good morning, Marshal." He waved for me to follow him, then he led the way back to his desk on the easternmost side of the office building. He gestured to a ladder-back chair. I sat while he did the same on his side of the desk.

He leaned forward with elbows on the smooth top. "Did you get permission to stay?"

"I did. I'm officially on the case."

He breathed a sigh of relief. "How would you like to proceed?"

I held my hat in my hands. "I've been thinking about that." I pointed toward the smelter buildings. "The first thing I'd like to do is get a look see at the ingot room to find out where the ingots are stored, how they are moved and where they might be hidden." I leaned forward. "I assume you are best suited for that? After all, you are the only one besides Mr. Marks with a key."

He started to stand. "We can go right now."

I motioned for him to retake his seat. "Then I'd like to get an idea of your operation here. I'd appreciate it if you could arrange for someone to walk me through the building and explain how things work. After that I'd like to see the pulleys that broke loose and killed Peter Trudeau, and I'd like to speak with the same workers you interviewed who explained there was no one else in the proximity when the accident happened."

"That will not be a problem. I'll introduce you to William Huish, our operations chief. He knows more about smelting than any man in the territory. He can walk you through the smelter and I can show you the pulleys." He looked at me with a small smile. "Anything else?"

"No."

"Then let's go to the ingot room." He stood. "We can walk there right now."

Chapter 6

He stepped out the back door where we'd had our conversation the afternoon before. Together we walked down the powdery, dusty trail alongside the wood yard to the ingot room. As he did the day before, he removed the padlock and opened the door only enough for a man to enter.

He reached for a lantern and lit it, then waved his hand to the interior of the huge room. "We call this the ingot room, but in reality the ingots are kept next to the abutment at the base of the smoke stack." He pointed, first toward the smelter then toward the center of the room where the casket rested. "We initially stored them in the center there, but that turned out to be cumbersome and somewhat risky. Now, after each ingot cools, it is lowered to a stack next to the stairs where they stay until shipping days."

He led the way to the edge of the room closest to the smokestack and when he raised the lantern, I could see a dull glow return from the blocks stacked there. I jerked when I realized that I was looking at gold ingots, at least twenty of them, rectangular blocks roughly six inches on each side and twelve inches long. A low whistle escaped my lips as I thought of the value of the cubes so casually stacked in front of a set of wooden stairs in the large room.

Livingston irreverently tapped the lowest level with the toe of his boot. "These are gold ingots. They are not pure gold, of course, but they are nevertheless each worth in excess of eighty thousand dollars."

I shook my head. I'd never been in such close proximity to even a fraction of that much wealth. I turned to look up the stairs to the base of the smokestack fifteen yards away and wondered at the missing ingot. If it had been my gold, I'd make sure it was constantly guarded. I peered over my shoulder into the darkness of the cave-like room, but saw no one. I pointed up the stairs. "What keeps the wagons from that side from loading up and stealing you blind?"

He stared toward the furnace then turned to me. "This retaining wall is built to separate the two buildings on the east and west sides." He tapped the stairs. "The smelting floor is actually twenty feet higher than where we are standing. Obviously, no wagon can cross the drop off and certainly wouldn't be able to get back out that way."

I looked again. "Then how are the wagons

loaded when you ship the gold?"

He stepped to the space under the stairs. When he held the lantern close, I could see several two wheeled carts chained and padlocked to the rough-cut stair treads.

Livingston reached and touched one. "We use these to get the ingots from here to the pulleys in the middle of the ingot room. We only load on designated days, and like I told you, every wagon that comes in is searched on the way out to make sure they are leaving with exactly what the manifest says." He rattled the chain. "And we keep these locked to make sure they can't be used except on shipping days."

I nodded then looked again at the stack of thick, cubic ingots. Out of curiosity, I reached to try to pick one up. I'd always prided myself on my strength and assumed I'd be able to lift the metal. Small extensions protruded from each corner so I grasped two and strained. I could only lift it a few inches before letting it fall back with a solid clunk.

Livingston watched my effort with a smirk. "Only a few men here at the smelter are strong enough to lift one of those. They each weigh close to three hundred pounds." He pointed over his shoulder to the workers nearer the furnace. "That's why we don't keep a guard here at all times, because without the carts, they aren't going very far."

I stood and stretched my back. The ingots seemed small in comparison to their weight and their worth. I studied the stack with a frown. "But one did."

He grunted. "Yes, one did. I'm sure it is still close by."

"How do you stack them?"

"Come on. I'll show you."

Because of the increasing light, he blew into the lantern to extinguish the flame and placed it on a barrel at the foot of the stairs. He led the way up the steps while I followed. When we got to the landing, he pointed overhead to a block and tackle assembly attached to the rafters of the room. Ropes hung heavily, then curved to where they attached to a sidewall. Together we walked to that wall where he held the light to show me a set of wood and metal pulleys from which extended four small hooks.

He frowned and pointed to an empty, concrete floor close to the base of the smokestack. "These are the pulleys that broke loose and hit poor Peter in the head. He died right there on the cooling floor."

"What's a cooling floor?"

"It's where the molten gold is poured into a mold. It takes almost two days for it to cool enough to be moved." He tapped the pulleys. "These hooks attach to the ears on the ingots then we can lift them with the block and tackle. There is an identical block and tackle set in the center of the ingot room that we use to load the wagons."

I glanced into the darkness toward the center of the ingot room. All I could see was the thin stream of light entering through the small opening at the big door we'd squeezed through an hour earlier. I thought of the dead man, then glanced again at the pulleys. They were tied to the wall with a thin rope, and it was immediately easy for me to recognize how it could have broken or come untied. My initial conviction that a murder had taken place began to weaken.

My thoughts returned to the missing ingot. I stepped to a barrier rail in place to keep anyone from falling over the side. I motioned toward the stack on the floor. "You said when it is time to send them out, the ingots are moved with the hand carts from the bottom of the stairs to the center of the ingot room." I motioned with my head to the darkness of the big room. "From there they are loaded on the wagons. How often does that take place?"

"Depending on the richness of the ore, we can process approximately five ingots a week. Every three weeks to a month, we send a shipment to the train station to be taken to Philadelphia for further processing and refining." He pointed to the partially open door. "Each wagon that leaves through that door is searched and our records are carefully matched so we know exactly how many ingots are leaving. In the meantime, we keep a close watch on the ingots stored at the base of this wall. We've never had a discrepancy until a week ago."

We heard yelling from the men at the furnace. I wondered if something was wrong but Livingston seemed unconcerned. He stepped toward the commotion and bade me follow.

"They are getting ready to do a pour. You'll be interested in how it's done."

We strolled to the floor and I saw men scurrying here and there. Most wore no shirts and sweat glistened on their backs in the suffocating heat close to the fire pit. I rubbed my finger under my collar and tried to breathe.

Livingston propelled me forward until I could see a tall man with shoulder length hair and a long, white beard standing on a raised platform gesturing with his arms and hollering at the men. His shirt was open to the waist and the sweat on his chest glimmered in the light of the overhead holes in the roof. He looked like a picture I'd seen as a youngster of Moses standing on the mount calling the Israelites to repentance. I glanced at the men rushing with fear to obey every command and decided that the comparison was reasonable.

Livingston leaned close so I could hear over the din.

"That's Will Huish." He strode toward the tower so I followed.

We climbed to a platform immediately below the shelf on which the man stood. From our vantage point, I saw a worker reach with a long tool to turn a latch on the bottom of a huge cauldron. When he jerked the pole away, a red orange stream of molten metal escaped through a metal tube into what looked like a small, stone box. As it filled, the worker reached out again to close the latch, then the screaming from above instructed another man to unbolt the other side. I could barely see, but it appeared that another, much larger stream escaped from the opening on the opposite side into a rock channel that went through the outside wall.

Livingston turned to me with a loud voice. "And there you have it."

"Have what?"

He pointed to the small box. "Three hundred pounds of mostly pure gold." He then pointed to the wall where the molten river had escaped. "And three tons or more of slag."

Huish climbed down to our level and I realized that in close proximity he seemed even more Moses-like. He greeted Livingston and eyed me up and down. I tentatively extended my hand, unconsciously hoping I wouldn't get a shock. I leaned forward so he could hear. "Branson Hawk."

The handshake was firm but wet because of the sweat on both of our hands. Livingston turned to the steps, and with a wave over his shoulder, ordered us to follow. He led us away from the furnace through the huge gate where the ore wagons entered. Several waited just outside the gate with the big draft horses hanging their heads in restful inaction.

We stopped when Livingston turned, then he looked to Huish and used a normal voice because we'd left the noise behind.

"Marshal Hawk will take a few days to investigate the death of Peter Trudeau."

The bearded man turned his dark eyes to me before returning his attention to Livingston. "I thought you decided that was an accident?"

"I did and I continue to think it was, but a man is dead and Hawk has agreed to look into the matter."

Huish shrugged. "Very well. Do what you want. It has nothing to do with me."

"Well, I was hoping you'd show Marshal Hawk around and answer any of his questions."

Huish frowned at the annoyance. "Not this morning. We have too much to do to get ready for the next melt." He pointed to the wagons, piled high with rocks, waiting patiently to enter the big door. "We have to get this ore into the stamp mill to be broken up then into the vat for heating." He turned to me. "Maybe later this afternoon?"

I nodded. "That will be fine."

I pointed back inside. "Right now I'd like to talk with the three firemen Mr. Livingston interviewed. Can you have them meet me at the pulleys?"

"I'll send them right away." He glanced through the big door to the dark interior of the building. "Now, if you'll excuse me, I've got a lot of work to do."

After my nod, he started toward the oversized door. I watched him go and when he got inside, I immediately heard him screaming orders to the men.

Livingston must have read my thoughts about the man being unfriendly. He glanced at me with a smile. "He takes a little getting used to, but he's a good man. I'd trust him with my life."

I nodded. "That's high praise."

He smiled wider. "Yes, it is. But I mean it." He took a step toward the building. "Shall we go meet the men?"

The inside of the building seemed extra dark after having been in the bright sunshine. We took a moment for our eyes to adjust, then I followed Livingston to the north wall. I scanned the rope rising from the pulleys at the wall to a block and tackle mounted directly above where the gold ingot rested on the floor. The pulleys were tied high on the wall and I could see if they were released, they would swing toward the center of the floor with ever-increasing speed and would do irreparable harm if anyone happened to be in the way. I swallowed as I thought of the dead man, Peter, and the damage I'd seen on the side of his face the morning before.

I stood on a bench and studied the small rope holding the pulleys snugly against the wall, then turned to look at the cooling ingot on the floor. I touched Livingston on the shoulder, leaned down to his ear and spoke loudly. "Can we untie this and let it hang over the ingot?"

He stepped onto the bench and reached to tightly grasp the pulleys. "We need to make sure to hold them so they don't swing."

While he held the pulleys, I untied the thin rope, then together we stepped down and walked the pulleys to let them hang over the freshly poured ingot. We'd no sooner got there when three, shirtless men approached.

Livingston turned to me and took a deep breath so he could yell over the noise of the furnace. "Hawk, this here is Pablo." He pointed to the biggest of the men, then waved his hand at the others. "And this is August and Slim."

I stepped close to the trio. "Howdy, men. I'm U.S. Deputy Marshal Branson Hawk and I'm here looking into the death of Peter Trudeau. I understand you are the men who found him."

They nodded.

"Did you see the accident?"

Pablo cocked his head back toward the firebox and said something but I couldn't hear so he started to repeat. I held my hand out to stop him then leaned to Livingston with a loud voice.

"Can we go back outside so we can talk?"

We all walked to the big door that was opened wide to allow the ore wagons inside. We walked fifty yards away where I stopped and turned to Pablo.

"You didn't see what happened?"

He shook his head. "No. We heard a scream and hurried to the cooling area and saw the dead man."

I looked at the others. They nodded in agreement.

"Tell me what you saw when you got there."

The three men glanced at each other, then Pablo pointed over his shoulder with his thumb. "He was laying on the ground with the pulleys swinging over him. He touched one of the other men. "Slim and me tried to help while August ran to tell Huish."

"I see." I closed my eyes and pictured the area. I could see in my mind, Peter laying on the dirt with the pulleys swinging over him. "And you saw no one else."

He shook his head.

I tapped my foot. "Was Trudeau alive when you found him?"

"No. His face was smashed in and he wasn't breathing."

I chewed the inside of my lip while thinking. I looked up. "Do you think the scream was his?"

Pablo looked to the other men, then shrugged.

I wondered at the possibility that Trudeau had been killed and then brought to the cooling area to make it appear as though it had been an accident. I glanced at the men again. "Can you see the cooling area from your work station?"

Pablo continued to be the spokesman. "No."

I found myself thinking about what areas of the smelter would have a view of the cooling area, and I was suddenly anxious to get back inside to see the layout. I nodded my appreciation. "Thank you, men. You may go back to work now."

Livingston stepped closer and we watched as the men disappeared through the door. I noticed his glance toward the office building and realized that he must have work to do also.

I hitched my pants to my hips. "Mr. Livingston, if you have to get back to your office I can certainly continue on my own. I'd like to go back in and study the cooling area. Would that be all right?"

"I'm sure that would pose no problem as long as you stay out of the workers' way." He paused for a moment then waved his hand toward the building. "And remember, this can be a dangerous place, especially if you don't know your way around."

I looked toward the large door and the darkness within. "I understand."

We separated there, him walking to the offices and me back into the smelter. I strode directly to the cooling area where the pulleys hung unmoving, chest high above the hot gold.

I glanced to the fire tender's location around the corner and knew right away that no one there could have had a clear view of the accident, if it was an accident.

I studied the pulleys while tapping on a tooth with a fingernail. Something wasn't adding up but I couldn't put my finger on any discrepancy. I reached and pushed the pulleys away and watched them swing back toward me. I pushed again, harder. They swung away then came back. I tried to picture Peter innocently walking along before the vicious impact of the heavy pulleys.

My eyes snapped open. He'd been hit squarely in the head, but the pulleys were swinging only at shoulder height. I searched quickly to the thin rope on the wall, wondering if it was possible to tie the pulleys at a different height. It obviously wasn't. I thought quickly of the size of the man in the coffin I'd seen the day before. He had a thick chest and huge arms, but my most urgent question was suddenly how tall he was. If he was as tall or taller than me, he couldn't have been killed by accident.

I tied the pulleys back to the wall, taking extra care to tie the rope tight so they couldn't break loose and hurt someone. I retreated down the stairs to the ingot room and lit the lantern left there by Livingston. Holding it up, I walked directly to the tarp-covered casket, stepping ankle deep in the mud caused by the melting ice. Just as Livingston had done earlier, I slid the tarp to the ground then pulled the lid away. Even on the ice, the body was starting to decay and the smell was worse than the previous day. I pondered why Miss Trudeau was so intent on taking the body back to Santa Fe. A sister's love I supposed, and I couldn't argue with that.

I thought of how to best measure his height. I could see his boots touched the bottom of the coffin and his head was only an inch away from the top. I stood the lid on end and held it in front of me. I'm a fraction over six feet tall and the board towered over me at least six inches. There was no way the death could have been an accident. Now the question was, who killed the man? If I could learn the answer to that question, I had every reason to believe I would also know who stole the gold.

The mud sucked at my boots as I replaced the lid and the tarp. With the lantern held high, I decided to see where in the room a six-inch cube of gold might be hidden. I was sure that Livingston and Peter had searched, but a fresh pair of eyes might see something they missed.

Two hours later but no closer to an answer, I placed the lantern back to the post by the door and slipped out into the bright sunshine. I squinted for a moment and rubbed my eyes then walked on the path toward the back door to Livingston's office. On the way, I waved to the small, Mexican boy plodding along behind his father and the overloaded donkey.

At the back of the office building, I looked through the dirty window and saw Livingston sitting at his desk. I tapped. He jerked in sudden fright, but when he saw it was me, he relaxed and opened the door.

"Marshal Hawk, you nearly to scared me to death."

"Sorry about that." I pointed to his seat while I took the hard, wooden chair. "I'm convinced the death was a murder."

He sat up with a frown. "And how can you be so sure?"

"The pulleys."

Chapter 7

He looked at me with a puzzled expression.

"We untied them and let them come to rest above the gold ingot. When we did, do you remember how high above the ground they were?"

He pursed his lips as he thought for a moment. "About chest high."

"That's right. But Peter was hit in the head. The pulleys were not the cause of death."

He shook his head. "But the block and tackle assembly raises and lowers the pulleys. Just because they were chest high today doesn't mean they couldn't have been higher last week."

I leaned back and brought my fingers together like a tent, to my chin. "Precisely what I originally thought. But think about the rope and the ring on the wall the pulleys are tied to. If they were higher, they wouldn't be able to be tied to the wall because the small rope is too short to make the connection."

He gazed over my head and nodded slowly before looking back at me. "Then he was killed because he was looking for the missing ingot?"

"I believe so, yes." I sat up. "And because he was killed, you might also be a target. I suggest you stay out of the smelter buildings until I can bring the killer in."

His eyes opened wide and he swallowed. "And when might that be?"

"I'm hoping sooner rather than later. If we can find the ingot, we can find the killer, or if we find the killer, I'm sure we can find the ingot. Both crimes are tied together, which gives us the advantage. No matter where the clues lead, we will be closer to solving the murder as well as the theft."

He breathed deeply. "So, what is your next step?"

I had been contemplating that very question most of the morning. I leaned forward. "Huish will show me the smelter works this afternoon, but in the meantime, I have some questions."

He pushed himself higher in his chair. "Ask away. If I don't know the answer, we'll find someone who does."

"As I walked around today, I noticed many workers on the smelter level, but the whole time I was in the ingot room, not one soul could be found."

He nodded. "That's because the entire west side of the building is off limits to the workers. The only time they can enter is when Huish or Collins or one of us from the administration building accompanies them."

"Who is Collins?"

"He's Huish's right hand man. You saw him today. He's the one who opened the slot for the gold to flow into the ingot mold."

"I see." I tapped my fingers together in front of my face. "So no worker can go unless one of you are with him?"

"That's correct"

"It's a huge room and dark as night. How would anyone know if a worker slipped in there?"

He leaned back and crossed his legs. "Do you remember the platform Huish stood on today?"

"Yes."

"Either he or Collins is there whenever the smelter in in operation so they can make sure all goes well. Occasionally, when we are between melts, a crew is sent in to clean the ash from the combustion chamber, but even then, one man is always assigned to stand on the ledge. It is policy with no exceptions. That is the one place from which the entire building, east and west, can be seen. If any unauthorized person is caught where they don't belong, they are sacked on the spot."

I let my gaze drift through the window toward the smelter while thinking of my time there. "But I was in there alone for most of this morning. No one said anything to me."

He smiled. "That's because Huish knew you were supposed to be there, but you can be sure if not for that, he'd have sent the guards in and you'd have been harshly escorted out."

I tucked my thumbs into my belt. I was circling in on a thought but I knew it wouldn't set well with Livingston. I took a deep breath. "Then can we assume that the thief is from your most trusted group?"

His face grew suddenly pale. "It's not possible."

I sat up. "Why not?"

He stood and turned his back on me to look out the window. At length he rotated back toward me. "Because every single person who has access to the ingot room has been working here since the smelter was first built."

I watched his eyes as he slowly came to the realization that longevity in employment was no guarantee of an individual's honesty. He sighed as he retook his seat. "I suppose then, that I am on the suspect list?"

I looked him in the eye. What he said was true, he was on the list, but in his asking, I mentally removed him from consideration. I shook my head. "If you'd committed the crime why would you have told me about it? As far as I'm concerned, you are the only one not on the list."

He waved toward the other side of the office building. "Marks?"

I'd been thinking about that. He did request that I stay and investigate, but it could have been nothing more than a ploy to keep me from thinking of him as a possibility. I glanced up. "There is one way we can find out in a hurry. Does he have a private secretary?"

"Yes."

"If Marks was in on the theft, I imagine he would have changed his routine after inviting me to stay. Might you be able to ask his secretary if he's done anything out of the ordinary since yesterday afternoon?"

"I can easily do that." He pulled a gold watch

from his vest pocket and pushed the button to open the lid. "It's a quarter after twelve. He usually eats his lunch on the patio. I'll go there now."

"Excellent." I pointed toward the smokestack. "Huish said he would show me the smelter operations after noon. I'll go up there to see if now would be a good time. Can we meet back here at, say, four o'clock?"

He stood with a nod, then escorted me to the front door so I could walk to the smelter while he found Marks's private secretary. I was almost certain that he would find the man had done nothing out of the ordinary, but it would be good to know for sure.

The ore wagons I'd seen earlier were gone when I stepped through the big door into the room that housed the furnace. I glanced at the ledge to see Huish there. He saw me and waved unenthusiastically, then climbed down and met me at the base.

"I don't have much time."

The statement was short and to the point, but he didn't seem to be angry. I remembered our earlier conversation and his terse answers. I concluded that he did not mean to make me feel uncomfortable, rather, it was simply his manner.

Truth be known, after my talk with Livingston, I wasn't all that interested in the smelter operation. I was reasonably certain that the thief was not one of the laborers, rather, I decided to concentrate my investigative energies on the supervisory level.

"I promise not to take any more of your time than necessary." I peered up to the platform he'd been standing on." I pointed up. "Do you mind?"

He shrugged his indifference so I climbed the ladder to the very top. Livingston had been right, from the high level I could see almost every inch of the huge setting, although the cave-like ingot room was admittedly dark. I looked down and watched the fire tenders as they took turns throwing limbs through the small door, and I could see the raging inferno inside. Other workers shoveled any fallen rocks into carts then wheeled them to the opening of the ore bin.

Huish stood next to me on the platform. He knew I was investigating the death, but unless he was in on the theft, he didn't know about the missing ingot. I waved my arm toward the workers. "I'm told either you or Collins is on this scaffold every minute the smelter is in operation."

He leaned forward. "That's what Marks wants, so that's what we do."

I pointed to the ingot in the mold on the floor. "Then one of you would have been in a position to see the accident."

He uncomfortably shifted from foot to foot. "Well, sometimes we have to get down to check on things."

"Like when you came out to talk with Livingston and me this morning? There was no one here during that time, correct?"

His eyes squinted. "Yes."

"You were not on the scaffold when the accident happened, were you?"

He motioned toward the opposite side of the room. "I was at the stamp mill. There was a problem with one of the crushing cylinders." His expression grew defiant. "You can ask August. He came to find me to tell me about the accident. By the time I got there, the man was dead."

I thought of the conversation I'd had with

Pablo. He'd mentioned then that August had run to find Huish. I frowned. "Was it you or Collins who was supposed to be on the scaffold when the accident happened?"

He glanced away and I could see his jaw muscles working under the skin. He turned back. "Collins."

"I see." I tapped on the wooden safety railing around the platform. "So, it comes out that you and Collins are not always here? Did he tell you where he was?"

He clenched his teeth as he glared at me. "He said he stepped away for only a moment."

"Do you know where he stepped away to?"

Huish growled and waved his arm. "We have to keep this whole place running. We have quotas and time tables to meet and we can't do it all from the platform." He jammed his fists to his hips. "We stay up here as much as we can, but it's unreasonable that we be here every minute."

I could understand the man's frustration, but that didn't make him any less a suspect at the moment. I looked at him and nodded my understanding in hopes of reducing the tension between us. It worked because he relaxed his shoulders and turned to lean on the railing. I leaned next to him.

"Would you mind if I spoke with Collins?"

He stood straight and brought his fingers to his lips, then whistled. Several men looked up. He waved to one and motioned for him to join us.

I watched the man walk to the ladder and climb. When he stood with us, Huish gestured to him.

"This here is Jonas Collins." Without another

word, he grasped the ladder and climbed down.

Collins was three to four inches taller than me, a strapping, handsome young man with longish blond hair. I looked up into his face and reached out. "Branson Hawk."

He gazed at my hand, but instead of shaking, he raised his deformed right hand, which consisted of only a thumb and two fingers. My eyes were drawn to the scars and I inwardly shuddered. He lowered his hand and I looked down, suddenly aware that mine was still outstretched.

I pulled it back. "Sorry."

He glowered at me. "What do you want?"

I tapped my badge. "I'm looking into the death of Peter Trudeau."

His eyes narrowed to slits. "What about it?"

I looked to the ground twenty feet below and hoped he didn't get a hankering to throw me over the railing. "I was just wondering where you were when the accident happened?"

He stepped back and I was glad to see it. He pointed toward the ore wagon door.

"Over at the side."

"You were supposed to be here?"

His eyebrows pulled down and from his expression, I knew I wasn't making a friend.

"I had been here all morning. It wasn't my fault I was called away."

"Who called you away?"

"One of the teamsters."

Do you remember which one?"

He shook his head.

"Anyone else who would have seen you there when the accident happened?"

He lurched back. "Wait a minute. Are you

thinking I'm involved somehow? It was an accident." He jerked his thumb over his shoulder toward the pulleys.

I held my palms out. "I never said you were involved, but I have to ask these questions of everyone."

He calmed slightly, but it was plain to see he was not happy about my curiosity. He scratched his jaw with his mutilated hand. "I'm sure there were workers there who saw me, but I can't name one in particular."

I nodded then leaned on the railing with both elbows. There were other questions about the ingot room that I needed answers to, and I wondered if the big man would be willing to talk. I glanced to Collins. "I was told that when the smelter is in operation, either you or Huish is here on the tower all the time, but that obviously is not the case." I tried to soften the question in hopes of getting a truthful answer. "I know you can't do your job if you are constantly here, but can you tell me how much you are typically away?"

The soft approach didn't seem to work. He bristled again and answered quickly. "No more than a few minutes."

"Explain a few minutes."

"A few minutes is a few minutes. I might leave but I'm always back up here after only a short time."

I listened but was certain he was shading the truth. I was sure his, and probably Huish's, time away from the platform was considerably more than a few minutes. I took a disgusted breath. If that was the case, then the conclusion Livingston and I had come to about the thief and murderer being a supervisor may not have been true. It could have been any worker.

I gestured to my right. "While you are up here do you monitor what goes on in the ingot room?"

He glanced to the dark recesses. "It's pretty easy to tell if someone is there because it is so dark they have to have a lantern."

"I see. Have you seen anyone there in the past week?"

He frowned. "No. Only me and one of the fire tenders and we didn't go farther than the base of the drop off. We lowered a fresh ingot there earlier in the week." He motioned toward the new ingot. "We'll take that tomorrow night after it cools enough."

"Are you always the person who takes the ingots?"

"Yes. Me and one of the fire tenders because they work close by." He sucked air into the side of his mouth and used his head to motion toward the dark, cave-like room. "What does the ingot room have to do with anything?"

I felt a little better that he'd been willing to ask the question. At least I did until I reminded myself that as far as he was concerned I was only asking questions about Peter Trudeau. I waved my hand in dismissal. "I'm only trying to get an idea of how this place runs."

He seemed content with my answer, then glanced down. "If that's all, I have work to do."

"By all means. I don't want to hold you up."

He started down the ladder. I leaned over the opening. "Would you mind if I came with you tomorrow when you move the ingot?"

He shrugged. "Whatever you like."

Chapter 8

I continued leaning on the safety rail while I watched him join the workers below. I stood in the heat watching for at least fifteen minutes. It was enough time for me to confirm that the tower was probably unoccupied for a good deal more time than they had indicated. I frowned. If that was the case, my list of suspects grew once again to include everyone at the plant.

I wiped the sweat from my eyes and ran my finger around my collar, then climbed down the ladder and joined the fire tenders. Pablo looked up with a pleasant expression.

"Hello Pablo." I pointed to the others. "Which one is August?"

He whistled. Both men turned. Pablo waved for them to join us and they walked over. He pointed to the smallest of the men and yelled above the noise.

"August." He then motioned toward me with his head.

August stepped closer and I encouraged him to walk outside with me. Once out the door into the pleasant coolness, I turned.

"August. When the accident happened, you hurried to find Huish. Is that correct?"

"Yes, sir."

"Where was he?"

"At the stamp mill on the second level."

I removed my hat and wiped my brow with my sleeve then replaced it with a nod. "Thank you, August."

I watched him retreat, his stringy muscles showing under the skin of his bare, sweat-streaked back. I grunted at the thought of at least fifty men working in the smelter and the likelihood that any one of them might be desperate enough to attempt to steal a fortune, even if it meant killing a man. His acknowledgement that Huish had been at the stamp mill eased my mind considerably. I wouldn't rule the man out yet, but he was shoved considerably down on my mental list of suspects.

The winter breeze felt good as I walked slowly back to the office buildings. The time for my meeting with Livingston was still an hour away, but I was hoping he'd have found out about Marks so I could go back to town. I'd done all I could at the smelter that day. At this point in time, I knew enough about the operation so a tour wasn't necessary. I was sure that the knowledge of a U.S.

Marshal investigating a death would be all over the smelter and if the thief had killed once, I assumed he would not hesitate to kill again. If I became a target, I'd be ready, and if he showed his hand, I'd show mine—and I held the trump card in the way of the .45 on my hip.

There was another reason for my impatience. After learning what Livingston found out, I wanted to spend the rest of the afternoon with Miss Trudeau. I held my grin as I thought of her. She would load her brother on the train at ten o'clock the next morning to begin her trip back to Santa Fe, but until then I had every intention of spending as much time with her as possible.

I entered the main office building door and caught the attention of one of the clerks. He stood, but I motioned for him to retake his seat. "I know my way back to Livingston's space. Is it all right if I walk back?"

He hesitated and raised his eyebrows, but gestured toward the back in permission for me to proceed.

"Thank you." I walked past the desks until I reached Livingston.

He glanced up, then quickly stood as I approached. With a nervous expression, he opened the back door and pulled me outside. We walked down the deep, foot-worn path leading to the ingot room. When we were thirty feet from his office, he turned and looked around. Satisfied that no one could hear, he motioned toward Marks's office. The words boiled out of him so fast that I couldn't follow what he was trying to tell me.

I held my hands out. "Whoa there, friend. Slow down."

He took a quick breath and rubbed his hands together. "Allred told me that Marks made a quick, unexpected trip to town yesterday immediately after speaking with you. He said he was agitated about something and needed to send a telegraph message."

I looked to the east with a furrowed brow, gazing to the boulder-covered Dragoon Mountains in the background and the tops of the cottonwood trees on the San Pedro River bottom in the foreground. I thought of the previous day. After leaving the smelter, I had gone directly to the telegraph office, but I hadn't seen Marks. I absently rubbed the stubble on my chin. "Anything else?"

He smirked. "I hope to shout. Allred said that a courier came this morning to deliver a telegraph message, and when Marks saw it he was furious."

"Did he say what the message was?"

"No, just that whatever it was put Marks in a foul mood."

I turned to see the windows to Marks's office. Nothing Livingston had said was proof positive, but it sure put me in the mind to investigate the man further. If anyone was in a position to pull off a theft of that magnitude, it would be the manager of the entire operation.

I thought of a few of the other men I'd met in the previous two days. Huish was an interesting character, but Angus, the fire tender, had corroborated that he was out of the area when Peter was murdered. Jonas Collins had verified that the oversight ledge, which was supposed to always be occupied, was actually empty at least part of the time. I wondered who could have paid enough attention to murder Peter when no one was watching. And I also wondered about the man with the deformed hand.

I pointed over my shoulder to the smokestack. "Tell me about Collins."

Livingston glanced at my pointing and raised his eyebrows. "Don't know a lot about him other than he's been Huish's right hand man since the smelter opened. He's a private feller, keeps to himself, but the workers seem to respect him."

"What happened to his hand?"

Livingston sucked a quick breath. "A terrible accident. He'd opened the gold door to pour an ingot. When he started to close it, the rod broke as he was putting pressure on the latch. He stumbled forward and the bottom part of his hand splashed into the melted gold." Livingston shuddered. "He rolled away and pulled it out but only after half of his hand was burned away."

I swallowed at the thought of the unbelievable pain and involuntarily flexed my hand into a fist. "And he's still working?"

He nodded. "A tough hombre."

Without thinking, I rubbed my right hand with my left until I noticed Livingston watching me. "It makes my hand hurt just to think about it."

A sad smile came across Livingston's face. He pointed toward his office. Marks had Collins assigned to my department while he was getting well. He's left-handed so he was able to do some bookkeeping until he was well enough to go back to the smelter."

My brow furrowed on its own accord. "You'd think he would want to stay as far from that as possible."

"That's the way you and I think, but in truth, he was not a good bookkeeper. About the only thing he could do well was write. His penmanship was as good as any I've ever seen."

"Hmmm." Interesting but it had nothing to do with the case. I folded my arms and leaned back. "He seems young to be Huish's right hand man. Do you know how that came about?"

He shook his head. "I don't think they are related, if that's what you are asking. When the company hired Huish, he came along and they've been working together ever since."

"I see." There again, it was interesting information but there was nothing there to be investigated further. I tucked my thumbs into my belt. "Might there be anyone else who would want Peter dead? We are assuming the theft and the murder are connected, but we need to think about the possibility that they are not."

He stared into the distance, then turned to me. "Not that I can think of. Peter was a lively man with lots of friends. I've never heard anyone say a bad word about him. He seemed big and clumsy, but when he got a pencil in his hand, he was magical when it came to ciphering."

I nodded at the answer and fell back to the conclusion that the murder and the theft were related. I thought of Livingston's comment about Peter's size and—. I looked up. "How much do you think he weighed?"

He gazed at me, confused. "I don't know. I weigh about one hundred and seventy pounds and he was twice my size."

I stepped forward. "So in the neighborhood of three hundred pounds?"

"I suppose."

"And a gold ingot weighs in the neighborhood

of three hundred pounds?"

His eyes grew wide. "Yes."

I pointed to the ingot room. "We need to take another look into that casket."

Livingston pulled the keys from his pocket and held them forward, jangling them with emphasis. Together we strode to the big door. Once inside he lit the lantern and held it high while we hurried to the middle of the room. With him on one end and me on the other, we threw the tarp back then I stepped closer to slide the casket lid until it hung over and teetered to lean against the coffin.

With lantern held high, we stared with relief and disappointment at the body of the big man inside. Relief that he was there and no gold had been placed in his stead, and disappointed that he was still there and no gold had been placed in his stead.

I took a shallow breath and waved my hand in front of my face at the increasingly disturbing smell of death, and noticed Livingston doing the same. He looked at me and shook his head. I reached for the lid and had the casket half covered when I had a thought. I balanced the lid then stepped closer and motioned for Livingston to do the same.

"It's possible the ingot is hidden inside the coffin."

He held the lantern while I rolled Peter's body to its side. There was no gold hidden under the corpse and I found myself disappointed again. My boots made a sucking sound when I stepped back from the mud after replacing the casket lid. I stomped my feet to knock some of the clay off, then leaning from each end, we pulled the tarp back to cover the box and ice.

Once outside I breathed deeply of the refreshing, cold air. It was good that the body would be leaving the next morning. I shook my head and turned to Livingston. "I swear I don't know why Miss Trudeau is hell-bent on taking her brother back to Santa Fe for burial. Seems silly to me."

He pulled a handkerchief from his pocket and blew his nose. "I agree with you, but it's her brother and she can do what she wants." He replaced his handkerchief. "But I don't envy the porters who have to unload the casket when it gets to Santa Fe."

My lips pressed together at the thought. I gestured to the path and he took the lead with me following behind.

He spoke over his shoulder. "But you have to admit that she's a pretty little thing." He stopped and turned.

I inadvertently smiled, then brought my hand to my face so he couldn't see, but I was too late.

He chuckled. "I was wondering if you'd noticed."

"Hmmppff." I stepped around him and started toward the building. "Just offering my assistance. It's my duty as a sworn lawman."

He chuckled again, then hurried to keep pace. When we got to the door, I waited. He reached around me, pushed the door inward and encouraged me to enter. He stood behind the desk while I paused.

He cocked his head. "Odd that I never heard Peter mention that he had a sister." He sat heavily in the chair. "But, I suppose, all we ever talked about was work so there'd be no reason for him to mention her."

I shrugged then rubbed a finger inside my

collar and looked toward the front of the building. "Well, I'm going to town to check with the telegraph office." I smiled inwardly. I didn't want to tell Livingston that the real reason I was leaving was to see the beautiful woman. I couldn't get her out of my mind.

Chapter 9

I was able to catch a ride with a freight wagon heading back to Benson after a delivery to the smelter. The driver cheerily invited me to ride along and we chatted amiably until we reached the main street. I saw a barbershop with a sign adverting BATHS 25 CENTS. I grinned while I pointed. "That's my first stop."

He pulled the big horses to a standstill and I climbed down the front wheel then touched the brim of my hat. "Much obliged."

He raised one hand in a return gesture. "Any time."

The barbershop, empty in the early afternoon hour, was narrow and small with a single chair in the center and a small, potbellied stove in one corner. I nodded to the heavy, cigar-smoking man who sat in the chair.

He heaved himself to his feet. "Shave? Haircut?"

I scratched the lengthening growth of hair over my ears and glanced at my reflection in the mirror on the wall. I smiled to myself and turned to him. "Both after a bath, if you please."

He grinned and pointed through a curtain-draped opening. "Through there."

I removed my hat and hung it on a hat stand in a corner opposite the stove, then did the same with my long coat. He held the curtain as I ducked through the narrow opening. A copper tub, propped up on blocks, rested over a slatted, wooden floor.

The barber tapped the tub. "I've got a couple of buckets of water warming by the stove. I'll bring 'em right in." He exited while I hung my gun belt on a nail then removed and carefully folded my shirt, pants and long underwear.

When he returned, he poured the water into the tub, then retreated for the second bucket. I swirled the water with my hand, pleasantly surprised that the temperature was ideal. I stood and looked to the curtain and thought of the purse thief in Deming and of the advice I'd given Livingston to watch his back. I decided I'd better do the same. I pulled my .45 and placed it within reach on top of a folded towel on a bench at the side of the tub. Satisfied, I climbed in and waited for the second bucket.

The barber pushed through the curtain. "How would you like this bucket?"

I leaned forward. "Over my head and

shoulders, please."

He poured then stepped back. "If you'd like, I could wash your clothes for another two bits. It won't take much time and they can be drying by the stove while you bathe."

I combed my wet hair out of my face. "I'd appreciate that."

I washed my face and neck and rubbed my nose. I couldn't tell if the smell of the dead man was caught in my nose or if it was my imagination. I liberally used the oversized bar of lye soap and scrubbed with enthusiasm.

When finished, I dried with the towel, then wrapped it around my waist and stepped through the curtain. The barber looked at the pistol held in one hand, then raised his eyebrows and motioned to the chair. I took a seat. Thirty minutes later, I walked out of the shop bathed, clean-shaven and in clean clothes.

The telegraph office door creaked as I opened it and stepped inside. The same operator stood and raised his hand in recognition. I leaned on the counter with my left elbow while tapping my badge with my right hand. "Good afternoon. I'm here on official U.S. Marshal business. I'd like to ask you some questions."

He stared at me with an expression of indifference, then moved closer. "Sure thing, but I'll tell you right now that what's in any telegraph message is between the sender and the receiver. I forget them as soon as I'm done with them."

I placed both palms on the counter. I'd been impressed the day before when he'd allowed me to write my message in private, but now it appeared his attention to confidentiality was going to get in the way of my investigation. "You don't understand. A man's been murdered and what you can tell me will help me solve the case."

He lifted his palms to shoulder height. "Not my place to tell about any message. If you want to know, you'll have to talk to either the sender or the receiver."

I drummed my fingers on the smooth wood. It was obvious my badge didn't pull any weight with him, but I decided to try one more tact. "Even if the message had to do with breaking the law?"

He paused and thought for a moment, then shook his head. "I'm sorry. When I was hired, I was told to keep all things confidential. All things means all things."

I was frustrated but I had to admire the young man for being willing to stick to his commitments. I stood and tucked my thumbs into my belt. "Very well. Thank you for your time."

I strolled out of the small office and paused under the shade of the boardwalk overhang, looking left and right, up and down the street of the rough and tumble town. I rubbed my cleanly shaven chin and turned left to walk to the Occidental.

A bell rang above my head as I entered and the clerk stood from his stool. "Good day, Mr. Hawk." He reached behind him then slid my key across the counter.

"Thanks." I rubbed the key and stepped to the side to nonchalantly glance at the cubbyholes. I was gratified to see the key was gone from number six, which meant that Miss Trudeau was in her room. I looked up the stairs to the landing, then climbed while humming a tune.

At the door with the brass number six tacked

at eye level, I took off my hat and knocked lightly. Miss Trudeau opened the door and I was surprised to see her in a fancy, high collar, blue dress, and not the drab, mourning outfit she'd so diligently worn for the past few days. The mourning veil was gone and the blue color of the dress matched her eyes. I swallowed as I allowed my eyes to wander over the form-fitting dress.

She smiled shyly and stepped into the room while motioning for me to enter. "Hello, Mr. Hawk." She looked quickly away. "Please forgive me. I wasn't going out and didn't expect callers." She nervously ran her hands down the side of the dress. "I simply could not abide in wearing that dreadful black dress one more day."

I was tempted to let my eyes roam again but caught myself and gazed into her face. "I can't say as I blame you." I had planned on inviting her out for a walk, but after her comment about not going out, I changed my mind. I rubbed the felt of my hat while trying to think of something to say.

She pulled a chair from a credenza and slid it forward with a nod of permission to sit while she sat delicately on the bed. "I'll be taking Peter home tomorrow."

I nodded. "I know. You can count on me to help you in any way I can."

She breathed deeply. "You've been so kind." She looked down quickly and brushed the wrinkles from her dress. "I hate to ask, but I would like one more thing if it's not too much trouble."

I crossed my legs and placed my hat on my knee. "Anything you want. You just name it."

She gazed at me with the most beautiful, reserved smile. "I'd like to go out to the ingot room to formally close the casket. Would you accompany me?"

In my imagination, I could suddenly smell the dead body again and I was sure she had no idea of how uncomfortable that would be for her. "I'll do whatever you wish, but I have to warn you that the body is decaying. That's no place for a fine lady like yourself. If you'd like, I can take care of that for you."

She sat dejectedly and looked at the floor. Finally, she glanced up. "It's something I must do, no matter how unpleasant. But I'd like for you to be there. Would you be so kind as to make arrangements for a carriage for tomorrow morning at eight?" She brushed the wrinkles of her dress. "I don't know anyone else in this town. There is no one for me to turn to." Her shoulders sagged and she buried her face in her hands and sobbed.

I stepped to the bed and sat next to her. She leaned against me until the racking sobs subsided. She rose and reached for the towel next to the washbasin and wiped her eyes, then turned to me. "You are the kindest man I've ever met." She paused for only a moment, then sat next to me again.

It wasn't often I got a compliment from a beautiful lady. I didn't know what to say so I kept my mouth shut, The only thing I could do was stare at her profile as I sat next to her on the bed, and I felt as though I could stare at her all day long. When she reached and took my hand in both of hers, I felt my heart would explode with excitement and desire.

We sat in heaven-sent silence for a minute or more and I reveled in my good fortune. Finally, she took a deep breath and stood while pulling me to my feet. She wrapped her arms around my neck and hugged me, then favored me with a kiss on my cheek. I'd never met a girl like her and my heart raced like a hummingbird's wings. I turned my head, searching for her lips with mine, but she released her grip and stepped away. I reached for her, for I wanted to hold her close and I wanted her to know of my growing love.

She shook her head and backed away. "I'm sorry. You are so kind and I'm taking advantage of you."

I'd never been taken advantage of like that before and I wasn't minding at all. "Miss Trudeau, I—."

She put her hand to my lips. "Shhh." She looked into my eyes and I felt my whole body shaking. With the side of her lip nervously tucked between her teeth, she turned and opened the door. "Thank you for stopping, but I need to be alone." She wouldn't look at me but studied the floor like it held the secrets to the universe.

I didn't know what else to do so I stepped past her into the hall and turned, hoping she would glance up so I could see her eyes. If only she could understand how much I cared for her, she wouldn't send me out. She didn't look up, instead, she closed the door, and the click of the lock was loud in the stillness.

My heart ached and I wanted to stomp my foot. I suddenly thought of all the things I should have said, but had been too clumsy to say them. I took my hat off and wiped the sweat from my brow, surprised at how hot the hallway had suddenly become.

A man in a business suit stepped out of room eight. He stopped and looked at me with distrust as he locked his door and tried the handle. I felt foolish that I'd been standing in front of a closed door for no telling how long. I reached into my pocket for my key then marched directly to my door and shoved the key into the keyhole.

Once inside I flipped my hat to the bed and poured water into the washbasin. With a frown, I splashed the cold water on my face then dabbed with the towel. All I could think about was what I should have said or what I should have done. I didn't know how to act around women and I was positive I'd come across like a fool. I stood straight and took a deep breath while gazing at myself in the mirror.

I touched my cheek where she'd kissed me and suddenly felt better. She had kissed me of her own accord, and that had to have meant something. I then thought of her request for me to accompany her to the ingot room to seal the coffin. I smiled in anticipation and hopeful excitement that she did have feelings for me. I turned to the window to look into the street while shielding my eyes against the setting sun with my hand. I'd make the arrangements right away; it was the least I could do for such a fine lady.

The owner of the livery stable bent to untie the big doors to close them for the night. He stood then he turned with a pleasant expression. "Howdy."

"Good afternoon. I'd like to rent a buggy for tomorrow morning."

He smiled as he held his suspenders away with his thumbs and let them snap back to his chest. "Happy to oblige." He inserted his thumbs again and stretched. "Two seater with two horses will be three dollars for the day, the one-seater with one horse will be a dollar a day." When he finished talking, he released the material to snap for the second time against his shirt. It seemed to be an unconscious action, for he'd no sooner released his hold than his thumbs were finding the suspenders and stretching again.

"One seater will be fine. Only me and a lady on a fast trip to the smelter."

He cocked his head while looking me up and down. "You got business there, do you?"

I nodded then moved my coat enough for him to see the badge. "I do."

The suspenders snapped again. He leaned forward and squinted at me. "I hear tell there was a murder out there a week or so back." He motioned toward me with his nose. "You must be the marshal they brung in to find the killer?"

There it was. I'd suspected that the word was out, but now I knew for sure. I also knew that the killer, whoever he was, would be well aware that an investigation was ongoing. I'd have to watch my back.

There was no reason for me to confirm or deny anything about the case so I matched the stableman's stare. I figured the less I said, the better. I had started the whole thing by agreeing to help Miss Trudeau, the murder investigation came along after. I shook my head. "Just helping a lady." I looked inside the door. "Can I fetch the buggy at a quarter to eight?"

He leaned back and found his suspenders again. "Sure thing. I'll have the horse harnessed and hitched and you can be on your way."

I nodded and turned, then grinned as I heard the expected snap. After two steps I stopped. "Hey, mister?"

"Yeah."

"If I was to need a horse tonight, how might that work?"

He pointed over his shoulder with his thumb. "I have several available. Ever since the trains started running, I don't rent out as many as I used to. I can let you take one for six bits as long as you have him back by morning."

"I'll have him back by midnight or a little after." I fished into my pants pocket for a paper dollar. When I handed it over, he flipped a quarter in change.

"Do you want me to saddle him right now?"

"Not just yet. If you could have your night man saddle and have him ready for me, I'd be obliged."

He frowned. "No night man. You'll have to saddle him yourself."

"Fine. Just show me which one and where the saddles are and I'll come fetch him about ten."

He snapped his suspenders then turned into the barn. He put his hand on the horn of a saddle on a rack and patted it in a message to tell me it was the one I should use. He then stepped to a bay in a stall and rubbed between the horse's eyes. "Take this one."

"I'll do that." I looked around. "It'll be plumb dark when I come back. Is there a lantern?"

He grinned and pointed to a post with a lantern perched on top.

I nodded and smiled. "Pleasure doing business with you." I strolled out of the barn and turned toward the main street of the growing town. I was glad the stable man hadn't asked about my plans, not that I'd have told him anyway. But truth was that I was making them up as I went along. I'd tried to find out about the messages Mr. Marks had sent and received, but since the telegraph man was bent on keeping confidentiality, I had decided to make a visit to his office at the smelter to see what I could find out. If the head man was the culprit, I'd be justified in what I was about to do, and if the search proved him to be innocent, he'd be glad I'd done it.

Chapter 10

The sun had given its last wink over the mountains and darkness was fast approaching as I skipped onto the boardwalk on the west end of town. Horses crowded at the hitching rails in front of every saloon, and as I walked along, I looked through the windows at the men inside who held bottles high and cheered each other. One man grinned and waved me inside but I shook my head and waved my hand in thanks. My first order of business was to get something to eat because my stomach was so empty a whirlwind could have taken me three counties over.

The Occidental was ahead and if Miss Trudeau had been able to join me, that's where I'd have gone.

Since I'd be eating alone, I decided to go to the other end of town to an eating hall where I'd heard most of the smelter workers ate. As I approached, I saw a crooked sign with CARLITA'S crudely painted in white letters. There were two reasons for choosing the second-rate establishment. First was the savings. I could eat beef stew and bread for fifty cents where an Occidental meal would set me back at least three times that. The second reason was to hear the chatter of the smelter workers. I assumed they were like miners or cowboys, free with their talk no matter who was listening.

I found an empty spot between two men and stepped over the long bench to sit down. Both men grumbled but neither man moved to make any more room for me, but I couldn't blame them, for they had no room on the opposite side either. Carlita, a plump Mexican woman with graying hair tied tightly behind her head and errant wisps of hair hanging in front of her face, appeared at my side and plopped a metal plate down, then splatted a ladleful of stew onto it.

"Bread's on the table." She didn't wait for an answer but was gone to another patron and repeated the coarse action.

I reached for some bread and started on the stew, which was surprisingly delicious. The chatter around the table, while about the smelter, had nothing to do with missing gold or the death of Peter Trudeau. I ate in silence while trying to pick up any tidbit of information that might help me with the investigation, but gave up after an hour and another helping of the stew. With difficulty and amid curses from new men on either side, I extracted myself from the long table and bench seat.

I placed two quarters in Carlita's hand and patted my stomach as I strolled out the door.

I turned left. I had two hours to kill before I would saddle the livery horse and make a trip to the smelter. I wandered down the boardwalk until I reached the open door of one of the new saloons in town. A drunk man staggered out of the establishment, tripped and fell into me. At the exact instant I bent to catch him, I heard a gunshot from down the street and a glass lantern immediately above my head shattered and went dark. It didn't take a genius to know the bullet had been intended for me.

Heart racing, I pulled the drunk man into the street next to the horses tied to the rail. He sank to his knees and seemed content to stay there while I searched over the horses' backs for any sign of the shooter. I saw nothing in the darkening street until someone from a saloon near the shooter stepped out and hollered.

I saw a flash of gray clothing then heard the sound of running footsteps. I sprinted around the horses to the man who'd come from the saloon. He stood on the boardwalk peering into the distance, then turned at my hurried approach.

"What's going on out here?"

The open door to the saloon made for good cover so I ducked in, then encouraged the man to enter in hopes he could tell me what he'd seen. He stood at the door, unaware of the danger, so I reached and grabbed a handful of his sleeve and jerked him inside.

He fell to the floor, but with surprising speed, stood and doubled his fists. "Now you've done it."

The man charged before allowing me to

explain, so I did the first thing that came to my mind, I pulled my pistol and slapped him across his temple. He went down in a heap and lay still at my feet. I glanced up at his friends as they started toward me with revenge in their eyes. They stopped as I lifted my gun.

"Y'all hold on." I nodded toward the street. "There's a killer out there and I just might have saved this man's life. Believe me or not, I don't care. But I'm leaving here to try to find the killer." I took a deep breath then bolted out the door.

Another shot rang out and I saw the rifle flash and heard the thud of the bullet as it struck the saloon wall. I shot toward the stab of flame but had little hope that I'd hit anything because of the distance and the dark. I rushed forward, changing directions every few seconds so I would present less of a target. When I got close to where the last shot had come from, I crouched behind a water trough.

Men poured out of the saloons to see what all the shooting was about. They hollered and made such a racket that I never heard any retreating footsteps. I stood and dashed forward to the corner of a building and looked down the alley I was sure he'd retreated into, but no one was there. I waited at the corner, straining to hear anything that might indicate the assailant was close, but heard nothing more than dogs barking in the distance and men talking in the street. Finally, I straightened. The shooter was long gone, but with the shots he had taken, I had confirmation that Peter Trudeau had been murdered. Why else would someone be trying to kill me? I reloaded the empty chamber and slipped my gun into the holster, then walked back to the street and the gathering of men there.

A big man stepped forward with gun drawn, but I wasn't worried because with the aid of the light streaming from the open doors of the nearest saloon, I could see the glint of a star on his chest.

"What's going on here?"

I walked directly to him. "Name is Branson Hawk, Deputy U.S. Marshal out of Tucson." I pointed over my shoulder with my thumb. "A man took a couple of shots at me."

He followed my pointing and squinted in the dark. "Why?"

I hitched my belt higher on my hip. If we'd been alone, I'd have told him everything, after all, he was a fellow lawman, but others had crowded around to hear our conversation. I shrugged. "Can't say."

Someone started playing a piano in the saloon and with the action in the street finished, most of the men returned to their barstools. The sheriff's deputy glanced toward the saloon then returned his gaze to me.

"Did you come to Benson on a case?"

There are lies and then there are lies. Technically, I hadn't come to Benson on a case, I'd come to help Miss Trudeau. "No, I came to help a lady. Her brother was killed in an accident in the smelter and she came to take him back home for burial."

"I see." He nodded and rubbed his short beard. "And someone is trying to kill you for that?"

I turned toward the men standing close enough to hear the conversation, then reached to push my hat back on my head. "I can't imagine so, but you are a lawman, you know we all make enemies." I tugged on the lapels of my coat. "If you have a pot of coffee on in your office, how about we wander over there and talk about it for a bit?"

He glanced to the men and I hoped he'd caught my drift. He holstered his gun and motioned for me to join him in walking down the street. The men drifted back toward the saloon while the deputy and I strolled toward the sheriff's office. He stepped onto the boardwalk and through the door of a well-lit room, then pulled a chair and invited me to sit. I looked over my shoulder to the window then pulled the chair toward the other side of the room before sitting. He looked at the window then back to me and nodded, obviously understanding that I didn't want to get shot in the back by someone outside the window. I nodded and sat, crossed my legs and placed my hat on my knee while he hung his hat on a peg then poured two tin cups of coffee from a kettle on the potbellied stove.

The cup was hot and filled to the brim so I held it carefully by the handle and blew across the top. "Thank you."

He sat behind the desk and looked at me over his cup. His eyes bored into me and I suspected he wasn't impressed with my earlier explanation.

"Well?"

The scalding liquid was far too hot for me to sip. I valued the skin on my tongue more than the taste of the coffee. I leaned forward and placed the cup on the wood floor then stretched back and clasped my hands over my belt buckle.

"Truth is that I am here on a case, but I didn't want the whole town knowing about it."

"Go on."

I liked this deputy although I didn't know exactly why. I suppose part of it was that he'd seen through my half-truth but didn't make a federal case out of it. I sat up. I was in his town and quickly decided that he needed to know what I was working on. I told him the whole story of the missing gold and the murder of Peter Trudeau, and he listened without a single interruption.

When I finished he took a long gulp of his coffee then set the cup on the desk. "I'm glad you told me. It makes me feel a sight better about what I'm going to tell you."

I'd reached for my cup but stopped mid-motion and looked into his face. "What do you have to tell me?"

The deputy rubbed his palms on his pants. "I got a telegraph message from a sheriff up north. He says there's been talk of a shipment of gold to be delivered somewhere close to Denver in the next several days." He tapped his finger on the desk. "I'll give you one guess as to where that gold is supposed to come from?"

My forgotten coffee cup remained on the floor as I leaned back. I had a thousand thoughts racing through my head, but the one drumming the loudest was about George Marks. Of anyone at the smelter, my bet was that he was in the best position to get the gold out. He'd seemed anxious to find the thief and had requested my investigation, but his suddenly changed behavior and the new information about a gold shipment had my suspicion of him growing. I hadn't told the deputy about my planned visit to smelter office and I decided it might be best if I kept that to myself. But I was anxious to get in and poke around to see what I could find. In the meantime, I wanted some answers.

I held my fingers together under my chin. "Have you heard anything about anyone in particular who might be trying to get that gold away from here?"

He shook his head then tapped a tooth with a blunt fingernail. "No. I've been studying on that since I got the telegraph message, but can't come up with a reason to suspect anyone."

I tapped my fingers together under my nose. "My feeling is that it's not any of the folks who work there long hours for short pay. I'm thinking someone in a position of authority, one of the bosses."

He continued tapping his tooth. "You may be right. None of the peons would ever be able to steal enough gold to get my sheriff friend involved."

It was time for the question that I'd been grazing on for the past minute. "George Marks? It seems he would be in more of a position to steal than any others."

He leaned back with his hands clasped behind his neck and took a deep breath. With his eyes closed, he continued to breathe for a long moment. Finally, he opened his eyes. "It's not for me to say but..." He paused and frowned.

"But what?"

"It's only that most of the bosses are from around here and they have wives and most have children." He paused again.

"But Marks is not from these parts?"

He shook his head. "No. He was sent by the investors to run the place. He's from San Francisco as I recall."

My desire to take a look around his smelter office grew. "Do you know the man?"

The deputy studied the coffee in his cup as he swirled it. He seemed in no rush to answer my question. At length, he took another gulp. "Not more'n just saying hello if we happen to pass one another on the street." He looked to me as he set his cup on the desk. "He always seemed friendly enough."

"Can you think of anything in his behavior that might make you suspicious?"

He frowned. "No. He's a churchgoing man from what I hear and very generous when they pass the plate. I suspect the whole town would be shocked if it came out that he was outside the law."

I leaned back and ruminated on his statement. Livingston had said almost the same thing about Marks, but I wasn't quite ready to let go of him as a possible suspect. I reached and took my cup from the floor, careful not to spill it because it was brim-full. I blew across the top then took a sip.

"I've also met Livingston and Huish and Collins. What can you tell me about them?"

He tapped his tooth again. "I've talked to Livingston a time or two. Seems to be a straight shooter, but I've seen good men go plumb bad when it comes to gold."

I nodded. I had seen the same thing. "Huish?"

He grinned. "Old Moses? He's so honest that if he ever got robbed he'd tell the thief about the double eagle he had hidden in his shoe." He chuckled.

I joined in the chuckle as I recalled my first impression of the man on the smelter tower.

I took another sip of my coffee. "Collins?"

"Collins is an interesting man. He's been at the smelter from the first day and he caused quite a stir among the ladies in town when he showed up. He's so big and handsome, he could have had his pick, but he never paid the least attention to any of the single girls. Somebody said he had a fiancé up north somewhere." He grinned and cocked his head. "You have to admire a man who keeps commitments even though he had plenty of chances here to win a girl's heart." A gloomy expression replaced the grin on his face. "It was sad day when he burned most of his hand off. I can't imagine how painful that was."

The deputy unconsciously rubbed one hand with the other. With effort, I refrained from doing the same thing.

"After the accident he rarely comes to town. He keeps to himself at his little shack on the river north of town."

The chair creaked as I stood with my coffee cup in my hand. I had no specific reason to suspect any of the men we'd spoken of, but it had been good to hear the deputy's thoughts. I shifted from foot to foot. "Anyone else come to mind that might be in a plot to steal close to a hundred thousand in gold?"

He pursed his lips in thought. "I don't know any of them all that well, but I can't say as I'd look into one any more than the others."

I took one last sip then placed the cup on his desk. "Obliged for the coffee. I'll probably be in town a few more days. If you get wind of anything, I'd appreciate you letting me know."

He stood and reached for a shake. "And I'd like to be kept up to date also." He stepped around the desk. "You said something about helping a lady with her dead brother?"

"Yep. I'll take her out to the smelter first thing in the morning so she can close the casket. After that we'll make sure it gets to the train and they'll be off to Santa Fe."

"Well, good luck and keep me posted."

"I'll do that."

He opened the door and I stepped quickly to the darkness in the middle of the street, relieved that the shooter had not taken up station nearby to shoot me as I left.

Chapter 11

Staying as much as possible to the darkest locations, I made my way to the livery stable where I saddled the bay. After pulling the cinch tight, I slipped the bridle into his mouth and the headstall over his ears. He willingly followed me out the door then stood as I mounted. I pushed him south along the wide road used by the ore wagons. In ten minutes, I stepped down in front of the oversized office building where I noticed with satisfaction that no lights burned inside.

I tied the reins to one of the hitching rails at the side then strode to the main door and growled when I found it locked. Not that I'd expected it to be open with a welcome sign for anyone who might want to enter, but I'd been hopeful nonetheless. I walked to the other front-facing door on the other side of the building, but had no success there either.

I knew there were two doors at the back of the building. I had no pretenses that the one leading to Livingston's space might be open, for I'd spent time with the man over the last few days and I knew he was meticulous when it came to locking the doors. Nevertheless, I walked to it and pulled the handle. As expected, it was locked tight. I grunted before making my way to the last door.

To my surprise, it opened easily so I stepped inside and closed it behind me. I leaned forward, trying to see in the darkness. The minimal light from the half-moon showed only the outline of the desks in the big room, but that was enough for me to step around them and let myself directly into Marks's office.

Taking a chance, I raised the globe of the lantern on his desk and struck a match from a nearby box. The wick caught and when I lowered the globe, the room brightened. I sat at his seat, looking through the papers on his desk. They had to do with the smelter, ore loads in, and gold and silver production as well as expenses. I did no more than glance at them because they held no interest for me. Specifically I was looking for the telegraph messages he'd sent and received after my arrival.

The first drawer on the right held only a bottle of high priced whiskey and two small glasses. I'll admit to the temptation to pour myself a shot, but that was out of the question. The second drawer contained extra pencils, an ink well and stationary. I closed it and slid the bottom drawer open to discover a large ledger book. I hefted it and flipped it open to see page after page of neatly written numbers. They meant nothing to me so I moved on.

The top drawer on the left brought a smile to my face as I opened it. Stacks of telegraph pages completely filled the space. I reached for the nearest bundle and set it on the desk.

I pulled the string and released the bow which held the stack in place and almost giggled in glee when I saw that the messages included both those he'd received and also those he'd sent. And even better, they were organized from the most recent on top. I silently thanked the man for being so organized.

I quickly turned the papers to the day after Livingston and I had come to Marks with the news of the theft. I blinked when I found the first of the messages, the one that had thrown Marks into the rage that Livingston had learned about from the private secretary.

GEORGE MARKS, BENSON, ARIZONA TERRITORY

DISMAYED TO HEAR OF MISSING INGOT. FIND IMMEDIATELY OR ELSE.

THADIUS

I turned to the next message, the one Marks had sent.

THADIUS BROCK, SAN FRANCISCO, CALIFORNIA

THAD, ONE INGOT MISSING. U.S. MARSHAL INVESTIGATING

GEORGE

I held the paper in my hand and rubbed it between my fingers. I could only assume that Thadius was tied in with the investors, and Marks had been quick to tell the man about the theft as soon as he'd found out. I tapped the paper on my thigh. If Marks had been involved in the theft, why would he let his employer know? The answer was simple in my mind, he wasn't involved and I breathed deeply in relief.

I glanced around, knowing that it would be best if I left, but I wanted to see what communications he'd sent and received at the death of Peter Trudeau. I turned the pages until I found four messages, two incoming and two outgoing. The first was to Thadius informing him of the unfortunate accident and a reply instructing Marks to do what he could within reason to comfort the family. The next was to Miss Trudeau expressing condolences and offering assistance, then a return message from her requesting the body be held until she could arrive to take him back to Santa Fe.

I leaned back and imagined the grief of the beautiful woman as she read the message that her brother had been killed. How devastating that must have been. I vowed again to help her in any way I could.

With the messages replaced, I retied the bow and set the bundle back into the drawer. I looked around, wondering if there was anything else I needed to see, but decided there was no reason for me to stay. I closed all the drawers and took a moment to make sure I'd left no signs of my intrusion. Satisfied, I stood and leaned to cup my hand at the lantern's chimney and blow out the flame. I waited for a moment to let my eyes adjust to the darkness, then carefully made my way out of the office and to the door.

The bay knew he was heading home so he

tugged at the bit. I held him at a steady half-trot and rode directly to the livery stable, where I rode inside and fired the lantern. I was pleased with my night's work. The colonel might not have approved, but I'd found what I needed to know. I knew I could trust Marks and that alone made me feel much better about the case.

I entered the Occidental a little before midnight. A new night clerk stirred then stood and squinted. I felt a little remorse that I'd woken him.

"Sorry about coming in so late."

He waved his hand in front of his face. "Perfectly all right." He waited until I told him my name and room number then he slid my key across the counter.

"Thank you, friend."

He smiled and retook his seat on the stool and folded his arms. My guess was that within a few minutes he would be dozing again. I climbed the stairs and smiled to myself in anticipation as I passed room six. I'd have breakfast with Miss Trudeau, then take her to the smelter. As I got to my room, I turned the key then stepped quickly to the side as I pushed the door inward in case whoever had been shooting at me had decided on an ambush. Relieved at the silence in the room, I entered and hung my hat on the rack. After I washed my face and climbed into the bed, I wasn't surprised that it took only a few minutes to drift off to sleep.

The light of dawn crept through the window and bathed my room in early morning softness. I opened one eye, then the other, and rolled to sit on the bed. Breathing deeply, I rubbed my hands across my neck and shoulders, then stood to wash my face.

I peered out the window to the deserted street and smiled as I got dressed. I pulled my pants and shirt on, tied my string tie and brushed my boots before pulling them on. This would likely be my last meeting with Miss Trudeau and I wanted it to be perfect. I stood and studied my reflection in the mirror, then with one last adjustment of my collar over my tie and a vain wink at myself in the mirror, I stepped out the door and turned toward her room.

Her small, gracious smile behind the veil warmed my heart when she opened the door at my knock. She had resumed the mourning attire and I found myself wishing she'd worn the blue dress I'd seen the day before. I held my arm for her. "We'll have breakfast, then I'll accompany you to the smelter."

She grasped my arm above the elbow and we walked side-by-side down the carpeted stairs to the lobby and into the connected restaurant. I held her chair as she sat and she rewarded me with a nod.

"You are too kind."

I slid into my chair on the opposite side of the small table and stared into her face. She looked away in embarrassment then fiddled with the handbag I had rescued on the train four days earlier.

A waiter glided to our side and we ordered. We watched him retreat, then we waited in distracted silence. With her gloved hand, she drew imaginary lines and circles on the linen tablecloth and seemed in no mood to talk. I honored that and sat quietly, occasionally stealing glimpses of her face. When the food arrived, she ate daintily, reservedly picking at the eggs and bacon. I, on the other hand, ate all on my plate and contemplated asking if she'd be willing to share hers. No sense in letting good food go to waste.

At last she placed her fork next to her plate and delicately wiped her lips with the cloth napkin. She folded it neatly and placed it next to her fork, then looked up at me with the most lost and lonely eyes I've ever seen. My thoughts of her food turned to thoughts of her.

She fiddled with her veil, pulling it down now that she had finished eating. She leaned back and looked at me. "This is not something I'm looking forward to."

I didn't know if she was referring to closing the casket at the smelter or the trip home, but I nodded and reached both hands across the table. She glanced down then placed her hands in mine. I could scarcely breathe. She sighed then pulled her hands away and held them on her lap.

I wanted to sit and stare at her for hours, but I knew I couldn't. Besides, she got nervous whenever I gazed at her and I thought again of her comment about the hungry wolf. I stood. "We should go now." I moved to pull her chair as she stood.

She took a deep breath and pushed up from the table, then turned and grasped my arm for support. I placed my hand on her waist and held her for a moment as she regained her composure.

Her eyes were moist as she bravely looked ahead. "Shall we go?"

We walked together in the cold, morning air and I was impressed with her fortitude in the face of the unpleasant ordeal. As we approached the livery stable I saw the owner standing next to a single-seat, one-horse buggy with a fringed top. He watched the woman, then, with what I took to be an envious smile, he nodded toward me. He had every right to be envious, and I confess, I puffed my chest as I read his nod.

I held Miss Trudeau's hand to help her into the buggy, then walked around to climb in the other side. The stable owner stepped back and after a polite touch of my hat brim in his direction, I lightly slapped the long reins onto the sorrel mare's back. She started ahead at a pleasant trot.

The bright sun and warming air made the drive tolerably pleasant although there was no conversation. Miss Trudeau was content to sit in silence and I hadn't wanted to intrude on her thoughts. In ten minutes, I pulled the mare to a stop in front of the office building. I set the brake then jumped down and hurried to assist her to the ground. She took a moment to smooth the black dress over her hips, then after a deep breath, she boldly stepped forward through the door.

One of the clerks noticed us right away. He nodded permission for us to go back to Livingston's desk, so, holding her hand, I led the way. Livingston stood and hurried to meet us in the middle of the scattered desks.

He reached for her hand and lightly squeezed. "Miss Trudeau. A pleasure to see you again, although we all wish it could be under more agreeable circumstances."

"Thank you, Mr. Livingston." She released his hand then held to my arm. "I understand a wagon will be loading Peter's body in plenty of time to get to the train station. Is that correct?"

"Yes, ma'am." He pulled his pocket watch and flipped the lid. "It's slightly after eight now and the train leaves at eleven. We plan on having the body to the station by ten."

"And did Mr. Hawk explain that I am here to formally close the casket?"

She squeezed my arm and my mouth got suddenly dry. I resisted the temptation to reach and pull her closer.

Livingston glanced at me for an instant. "He did. We've been waiting for you." He turned his attention to her shoes and frowned before looking to me. "Mr. Hawk, I'll walk to the ingot room from here. I assume you came in a buggy?"

"Yes. It's in the front."

"Excellent. I'll not suggest Miss Trudeau walk through the dust. If you would please escort her in the buggy through the wood yard, I'll meet you there."

She and I turned and walked back the way we'd come. I nodded thanks to the clerk, then we exited the building and I helped her into the buggy. I clucked to the sorrel mare and turned her toward the path to the wood yard and the ingot room. We rode in silence, the only sound in the morning stillness, the rhythmic clip clop of the as the mare trotted along. Livingston waited at the partially opened door to the ingot room with a lantern, a hammer and small can tucked under his arm. He quickly placed everything on the ground to assist Miss Trudeau from the buggy.

He reached to pass the lantern to me, then retrieved the hammer and can from the dirt. As a group, we stepped to the door where he gestured for us to enter. I held the light high as we walked to the center of the room where the casket rested on the blocks of ice.

Miss Trudeau suddenly sobbed and dropped to her knees. Her hands covered her face and her shoulders shuddered at her sobbing. "I can't do this."

I reached to help her to her feet but she made no effort to rise. Livingston and I stood on either side and looked at one another for what seemed a long while, neither of us was sure of what to do, so we did nothing.

She raised her head and looked at me with tears glistening in the light of the lantern. "Mr. Hawk. Would you please close the casket? I don't have the strength."

I gazed down at her and could see her eyes pleading with me. With uncharacteristic slowness, I turned to Livingston. Holding the lantern for him to grasp, I took the hammer and small can with a handful of nails.

The mud from the melting ice had deepened and extended farther into the room from the casket. My feet sank to my ankles as I stood at the side. I turned to see her and him watching me, then without ceremony I set the can on the lid and pulled out the first nail.

It was much smaller than I'd expected, but I was no carpenter and realized I should have had no expectations. With relief, I concluded that the smaller nail would be less likely to bend, and in my limited experience, my nail driving was far from proficient. And besides, it wasn't like there was any worry that the lid could be pushed off from the inside.

I held the nail at the edge and started it with the hammer. I'd driven it only partially through the lid when I stopped. I looked back to Livingston, remembering how we'd checked the coffin to make sure no gold ingot was inside, and also thinking that to do so again was probably in the best interest of everyone involved. I was momentarily torn between the desire to protect Miss Trudeau, and my duties as a sworn lawman. I turned back to the casket and swallowed. With a push, I slid the lid to balance on the end then allowed it to teeter until it rested on the ground.

The smell was far from pleasant, but I was happy to see the body inside and no ingot there. I dared not risk a glance back at the woman for fear that she'd been appalled at my natural inquisitiveness, so I pulled the lid over the top and nailed eight nails, two on each end and two on each side. When finished, with the mud sucking at my boots, I stepped back, then turned to see Livingston and Miss Trudeau. I was pleasantly surprised at her relaxed expression of peace. Livingston and I each took an arm and assisted her to her feet.

She took a deep breath. "Thank you, Mr. Hawk."

"Think nothing of it. I told you I'd stay and help in any way I could. If you need anything you can count on me."

She licked her lips and touched my shoulder. "There is something."

"Yes?"

She glanced from me to Livingston. "May I be alone to sit with him for a time?"

It was a logical request from my perspective and I could wait as long as she needed, but it was Livingston's decision because it was smelter property.

He looked toward the door then back to her. "I don't see what harm it could do to have you stay here a while." He held the lantern higher and looked for anything to sit on. He found nothing and shook his head. "You can wait here. Any closer and you'll get your shoes muddy." He handed her the lantern. "Sorry there is no place to sit."

She waved the inconvenience away and we turned to the crease of light coming in through the door. We'd gone almost to the exit when she made another request.

"Would it be too much trouble to ask you to close the door while I'm here?"

We turned to see she'd already turned the lantern down low. If we closed the door it would be almost pitch black in the big room. I cocked my head, wondering why she would want it so dark.

She gazed at me then waved toward the coffin. "I'd like it to be dark. I'll be able to more intensely feel his closeness."

Livingston nodded. "Of course."

I squinted my eyes in the bright, morning sun as we stepped out. Livingston pushed the big door closed leaving her alone with her brother while I climbed into the buggy because it was the most comfortable place to sit and wait. I put my foot on the front rail and motioned toward Livingston's office. "I can stay here if you're needing to get back to work."

He stepped to the front wheel and rested his hands there. "When this door is unlocked, I'm usually right here. Surely she won't be too long." He pulled his pocket watch again. "The wagon is supposed to be here in half an hour or so."

I leaned back in the leather seat, put my other foot on the rail and clasped my hands over my belt buckle. I nodded toward the door. "I hope they are bringing some help to load the casket."

He clucked his tongue as he patted the front wheel. "They will use the block and tackle. That's why we put him under it to begin with. We used the gear to unload the ice blocks then put the casket on top. When the wagon gets here, they'll load everything and take it to the station. That's where the hard work will be. The men and porters will have to move the ice blocks to the freight car then put the casket on top."

I rolled my thumbs as I thought about what he'd said and decided that putting a heavy body under the pulleys was a smart idea. I looked toward the back door of the office building I had slipped through the night before and decided that with Miss Trudeau inside, this would be a good time to catch up on the rest I'd missed. I pulled my hat down over my eyes and settled deeper into the seat. I didn't expect to sleep, but it felt good to close my eyes.

Every few minutes I heard Livingston pop the latch on his pocket watch. I opened one eye under my hat brim and peered at him as he nervously paced back and forth alongside the buggy. Finally, I sat up. "Friend, you need to relax. Wearing your boots out isn't going to make her come out any faster."

He shook his head and placed both hands on the front wheel. "It's only that no one is supposed to be in there without someone to watch them."

I grinned. "You're afraid she's going to put an ingot in her handbag and walk out of there with it?"

He pursed his lips. "No, of course not."

"Then take a seat and rest your bones."

He stared again toward the ingot room then turned to me. "I'm far behind in getting a report ready for the investors. Would you mind terribly if I asked you to stay here and wait for her?"

I sat up and pushed my hat back on my head. "I brought her here and I'll take her to the station, so I'm not planning on leaving anyway. You go on and sharpen your pencils. Don't worry about a thing here."

He sighed then nodded his appreciation. With one final glance over his shoulder, he marched up the path to his office door. A few minutes later, I saw movement at the door and was happy to see Miss Trudeau sliding through the narrow opening. She paused and held her hands to her eyes because of the bright sunlight. I scampered from the wagon to take hold of her arm and guide her to the buggy where she sat heavily under the fringed, canvas top. I climbed in next to her and we sat there in comfortable silence for at least twenty minutes waiting for the wagon that would take Peter's body to the train station.

Chapter 12

We sat up when we heard a teamster hollering at the entrance of the wood yard. I stood in the buggy and watched the four-horse team and the plain, wood-sided wagon as it rolled closer and came to a stop next to the buggy. I recognized the teamster as he looked at me. He smiled then reached into his shirt pocket and held a plug of tobacco up for me to see. "Offer still stands."

I returned his grin and waved my hand. "Not for me, thanks."

He took the next quarter minute to stare at Miss Trudeau, but she didn't move and didn't look up from her concentration on the buggy floor.

He glanced at me and smiled as he replaced

the cube into his pocket and stood on the wagon bed. He pointed to the door. "Y'all ready to load?"

I shrugged because it wasn't my decision to make. I turned toward the office building, relieved to see Livingston marching down the path. I pointed. "There's your man."

Livingston strode directly to the big door and pushed it completely open, then motioned for the teamster to turn his team around and back into the cave-like room.

Livingston caught my attention, then pointed toward the smelter. He cleared his throat. "I'll go get some help for the block and tackle." He lifted the lantern and disappeared on the inside.

Miss Trudeau and I stayed in the buggy and peered into the darkened interior of the room as the teamster maneuvered his team. With the door open, the horses responded to the driver's skilled cues and in less time than I had anticipated, the end of the wagon stopped directly in front of the tarp-covered casket.

Almost immediately, Livingston returned with two men who skillfully used tie ropes and the block and tackle to load the casket. From somewhere, one of the men brought out huge ice tongs, which were used in conjunction with the block and tackle to lift the blocks one by one into the wagon. With the tailgate shut, the driver coaxed his team back into the sunlight and Livingston and the two men followed.

When they got to the light, I could see one of the men was Huish's right hand man, Collins. He stopped and stood directly outside the door and looked at Miss Trudeau and me, then turned back into the building and closed the door from the inside. Livingston pulled the chains through the rings and locked the gate then walked alongside our buggy.

At the gate, two men with rifles carried in the crooks of their arms met the freight wagon. The teamster pulled to a stop and the men looked into every possible space in the wagon where a gold ingot might be hidden. I knew there was no ingot for I'd watched Collins and his helper load the casket and the ice and nothing else, so I wasn't surprised when the guards climbed down and signaled the teamster through.

As we approached, the guards stopped us and looked the buggy over with equal scrutiny before waving for us to continue. Livingston nodded to Miss Trudeau, then stepped back to stand by the guards. I clucked to the mare and she responded by trotting to catch the wagon, which we followed to the train station.

As he'd done in the ingot room, the teamster expertly backed the horses and wagon to the loading dock at the station. Someone must have made arrangements because almost immediately, four porters climbed into the wagon with ice tongs like the ones I'd seen at the smelter. They unloaded the blocks of ice, placing them on hand carts, then with grunts of exertion, wheeled them to an awaiting baggage car on the other side of the dock. With surprising swiftness, they returned with small ropes, which they positioned under the casket. Each grabbed a rope end and lifted in unison.

They shuffled their way to the baggage car and we could see that Peter's weight made carrying the coffin awkward and difficult, especially when they attempted to enter the door of the car.

At last, with task completed, the four men exited the car and continued to load miscellaneous baggage and freight. From where we sat, we could see the tarp-covered coffin resting on the ice inside the car. I swallowed and inadvertently wrinkled my nose and wondered how the decomposing body would fare on the two-day trip.

Next to us, the tobacco-chewing teamster spat a long, brown stream of juice before waving good naturedly as he started his horses away. Within a minute, a smaller wagon arrived, backing into the same space.

The driver climbed over the seat and hollered at the porters. "Got two bags and a trunk from the hotel!"

One man rushed forward with a cart and placed the trunk with two bags on top then leaned to push toward the baggage car. I recognized Miss Trudeau's carpet-bag with the flower print. I took a breath and fought the urge to sigh. She was leaving and I didn't know if I'd ever see her again. I looked at her, hoping for a signal that she was feeling something for me, but she stared ahead until her bag disappeared through the baggage car's door.

Immediately, she stood and without assistance, stepped down from the buggy. She glanced up with a nod. "Thank you, Mr. Hawk. I'll not keep you any longer." She turned, and, holding the long dress up, climbed the steps and walked briskly past the caboose to the open door of the baggage car. She paused only briefly to look inside then hurried to the first waiting passenger car. Without so much as a backwards glance, she stepped aboard and disappeared from sight.

Her sudden actions confused me. I'd wanted

and expected something more in the way of goodbye, but in that blink of an eye she was gone and I sat alone in the buggy shaking my head. I wondered if I should have said something, anything. Maybe I should have told her that I had enjoyed the time we'd spent together or that I wanted to see her again. I stomped my foot on the floorboard. Why was I always so clumsy when it came to women?

Her abrupt departure was so uncharacteristic. She'd seemed so appreciative of what I'd done and gave me every impression that she'd enjoyed our time together. I was certain I wasn't mistaken about that, so I could only wonder if I'd done something to turn her so suddenly cold and distant. I could think of nothing amiss in my behavior. I'd been a gentleman. Awkward and clumsy perhaps, but a gentleman nonetheless.

I looked left and right as preparations were made for the train to depart. The porters rolled the door of the baggage car closed and the conductor walked along the platform calling, "All aboard to points east, Willcox, Bowie, and Deming." He stopped and allowed a scurrying passenger to run past and climb into the car, then he hitched his uniform pants and continued his strolling and chanting. "All aboard to points east."

Passengers scurried into the doors of the four passenger cars and within a minute, the connections between the cars of the train clanked loudly as the engine, with whistle blowing, jolted forward. I took a deep breath then leaned back with arms folded and placed my boots on the front rail of the buggy. As I watched the train pull slowly from the station, I began to wonder if perhaps Miss Trudeau's hurried departure may have had less to do with me than it was a result of her grief at the loss of her brother. With a spark of renewed hope, I smiled. That had to be it.

I stepped from the buggy and stood next to the chest-high concrete platform, leaning against it with my elbows resting there. I watched several people walk alongside the slow moving cars, waving and reaching to touch outstretched hands of departing passengers. Ever so slowly, the train worked to pick up speed.

From behind me, I heard creaking leather and turned to see the sheriff's deputy dismount with a nod.

"Morning."

I stood straight. The appearance of the lawman took my thoughts from Miss Trudeau and I suppose I was grateful for that. I shifted my gun belt. "Morning to you."

He loosely held his horse's reins in his beefy hand and placed his other thumb into his pants pocket while rocking back on his high-heeled boots. "Any luck with the missing gold?"

I pursed my lips. "Not yet." I pointed to the train with my nose. "The body of Miss Trudeau's brother is on the train. Now that she's on her way, I'll continue my investigation."

I looked beyond the end of the platform and saw the caboose a hundred yards away. I thought of the difficulty the porters had experienced when carrying the casket with the big man inside, and with a snap of my head, I instantly thought of my comment to Livingston that Peter weighed about the same as an ingot of gold.

I swallowed hard. It couldn't be! I'd personally nailed the coffin lid closed and had ridden in the buggy with Miss Trudeau from the smelter to the station. The freight wagon had never been out of my sight. There was no possible way anyone could have switched the body for the gold ingot.

My mind raced. With a sinking feeling, I realized that there had been a space of time between Miss Trudeau exiting the ingot room and the appearance of the freight wagon. Possibly as long as a full twenty minutes when the casket was out of my sight.

I stomped my foot and swore, then impulsively jerked the reins from the deputy's hand and in a single motion, swung onto the horse's back. "I'll be back in a bit." Without waiting for a response or permission, I kicked the deputy's horse into a sprint.

The big bay was game. I'll give credit to the deputy for choosing a good one. The horse stretched his neck and gathered the ground while I leaned forward to yell encouragement in his ear. A man, walking a lady toward town from the station hollered and shook his fist when I passed by with a cloud of dust. I glanced over my shoulder and saw them waving their hands in front of their faces, but a glance was all I could spare.

I was fortunate that there was a wagon trace next to the tracks. The bay gained ground on the level dirt, occasionally jumping a desert bush, but I knew the chase would be difficult because the train added momentum with each turn of the steam engine's powerful wheels. I rode like a wild man a hundred yards behind, pushing the horse and hoping we could catch the train before the river bridge only a half mile away. I kicked harder and the bay responded, running fearlessly along the side of the tracks.

We narrowed the gap to fifty yards but I blinked my eyes as I watched the big bridge grow closer and closer. Forty yards to the train, then thirty. The big bay was tiring but I couldn't let him slow down. Someone was trying to take advantage of Miss Trudeau. The poor girl. She thought her brother was in the coffin, but if I was right, a three hundred pound, six-by-six-by-twelve inch block of gold occupied the box, and she was none the wiser.

Twenty yards away, then ten. The engineer let out a long blast from the whistle as he approached the bridge and I knew I only had one chance. The big bay continued the sprint along the tracks but he'd given all I could have asked and then some. I looked at the bars holding the roof of the caboose and could feel the horse falter and I knew he couldn't continue. With all my strength I lunged from the saddle to take hold of the railings at the side of the caboose. I desperately latched on, hands clenched to the railings, but my feet dangled over the tracks. I tried frantically to pull up to find purchase with my knees but had no luck.

The open air grew suddenly confined as the beams of the bridge flew by only inches from my back. I dared not move because there was no room to lean out in an attempt to gain a foothold, but I didn't have the strength to hold on much longer. Finally, the bridge was behind me and with tremendous relief, I felt my boot gain hold. I pushed up with my leg until I found another foothold and was able to push over the handrail and onto the caboose platform.

I dropped to my knees and leaned against the bar, heaving in great gasps of air. I'd faced danger in many ways but that was the most terrified I'd ever been. I flexed my fingers as I leaned my head against the end wall of the caboose, too exhausted to move.

I rested there until I regained enough strength to push up from the platform. I stood and opened the door to the caboose, unsurprised that no one was inside for I'd been sure the conductor had gone forward to collect tickets from the passengers. A soft chair next to a pot-bellied stove looked inviting and though I stopped to linger for a moment, I withstood the temptation to rest. The next door opened to the between-cars platform and the door to the baggage car opened easily when I turned the knob.

I entered, fully expecting the windowless car to be dark, but was surprised when the first thing I saw was a lighted lantern resting on Peter's casket. Next to the casket, on a hard, wooden chair, Miss Trudeau stared at me with open-mouthed astonishment.

I nodded. "Hello Miss Trudeau." I stepped in and closed the door.

She stood. "What are you doing here?"

I tried to think of an easy way to tell her that her brother's body was possibly back at the smelter, having been switched for the stolen gold ingot. I was at a loss for words so I blurted it out. "I have reason to believe Peter is not in the box."

She frowned and hissed, then stood at the head of the casket and rubbed the wood. "Of course he's in there. You nailed the box closed yourself."

I stepped forward and placed my hands on the casket top. We stared at each other over the top of the coffin, barely eight feet apart. Her face was so childlike, so innocent. I swallowed, wishing I could hold her in my arms, to comfort her, to protect her. I longed to be able to spare her from the shock I was sure was at hand. It wasn't her fault that someone had taken advantage of her circumstances to get the ingot out of the smelter. She'd come with a noble desire to fulfill her duty as a sister and she had done that remarkably well, but I had to open the box and see for myself.

"I'm sorry, Miss Trudeau. I have to see what's inside." I held to the coffin for support as the car swayed back and forth and noticed her doing the same thing.

I looked toward each side of the car for something to pry the coffin lid away. It wouldn't take much, for the nails I'd used were only slightly longer than the top board was wide. I saw a shovel and reached to pick it up then started to insert the point under the top board.

I stopped abruptly when I heard the unmistakable sound of a gun hammer locking in place. I looked at the beautiful woman and the full-sized pistol with a wide bore pointed at my stomach.

"What are you doing?"

"I won't let you open it."

I suddenly understood. She was protecting her brother's memory. She'd come to take him home to give him a proper burial and I was somehow desecrating his memory by opening the sealed casket. I couldn't fault her. She was a fine woman, as fine a woman as I'd ever met.

I rested the shovel on the floor and smiled sadly. "I'm sorry, Miss Trudeau. I know this seems hard for you to understand, but if I'm right, Peter's body is not here."

"Then what do you think is there?"

Her voice was hard and cold and I felt guilty

that I'd put her in such an uncomfortable situation. Truth was, I hadn't expected her to be in the baggage car, although as I thought about the love she had for her brother, I shouldn't have been surprised.

I took a deep breath. "Someone stole a gold ingot from the smelter. I think whoever it was is taking advantage of Peter's death to get it out."

She slowly shook her head. "You're too smart for your own good."

I cocked my head. "What?"

"When did you know?"

"Livingston told me of the missing gold on the first day of our visit."

"That's not what I meant. We were so careful. Everything was planned down to the last detail. When did you know I was involved?"

I frowned as I thought about her question, then my shoulders sagged. I felt like I'd been kicked by a mule and I leaned against the casket. How could I have been so gullible to think I was falling in love—and my growing love for her had completely blinded me to what she actually was. I looked into her eyes and saw only hardness there. What should I have expected? I thought of her innocent questions about the smelter and how she'd originally thought it was a mine. She had been the consummate actress. The picture of the purse thief came to my mind. Had that also been part of her plan? She pulled me in so completely, playing me like a fish on a line. And I had been a willing fish.

I stood straighter. It was my turn for some questions. "When did you first decide to use me to help you get away with it?"

A dejected smile started at the corners of her

mouth. "Ordinarily I wouldn't answer that, but since you'll be dead in a few minutes, I'll tell you. Since you were so adamant that you accompany me, we decided to allow you to do so. What better cover than to have a Deputy U.S. Marshal as my personal escort. No one would suspect anything—and it worked to perfection." She pointed at the casket with the gun. "You are correct, the gold is in the box."

"And the hand bag thief on the train from Santa Fe?"

"Oh, that was certainly a nasty business. He did steal my bag."

"So, it wasn't part of your plan from the beginning?"

"Oh, my goodness, no. In fact, my original plan, after you so kindly returned the bag to me, was to get as far away from you as possible. I certainly didn't need a lawman hanging around. You'll remember that I did just that, telling you that as a genteel lady I had no sympathy for killers, but no matter how hard I tried to get you to leave, you always stayed." She shook her head. "Even here in Benson, I did all I could to be away from you, but your overworked sense of chivalry would not allow you to abandon me no matter how many times I told you otherwise. Finally, we decided that perhaps you could be useful, and you were. No one at the smelter suspected a thing because my special escort was a U.S. Marshal."

I shook my head. How could I have been so stupid? And all because of a pretty face.

The car swayed slightly and I held the casket for balance. I tapped the wood. "And Peter?"

She smirked and I realized for the first time

that she no longer wore the black hat and veil.

"I'd never seen him before. He was simply a man, and we needed man so when the gold replaced the body, no one would be the wiser. The hardest part was waiting for an accidental death at the smelter."

My eyes opened wide. "He wasn't killed because he was looking for the missing gold?"

"No. I didn't want anyone hurt, that's why we waited for an accident."

"It was no accident."

She studied me for a moment and waved the pistol. "You are mistaken."

I was confused. Peter had been killed, I was certain of it, but she, evidently, was equally as certain that he hadn't. I looked at the gaping bore of the gun and knew my own time was running short. My only chance was to keep her talking.

I wondered who her man was on the inside. He had to have been someone with access who could move freely. I gritted my teeth as I thought of the time she supposedly spent alone in her hotel room. There was no doubt that she and her accomplice had communicated to firm their plans over the past couple of days. How else could things have gone so smoothly for them? My eyes narrowed as I swallowed. "Who was your man on the inside?"

Before she could answer, the car jerked left then right on the uneven tracks. Miss Trudeau squealed and reached for the casket with both hands to keep from falling. That gave me the opportunity I'd hoped for. I'd seen the cotton cord running through small, metal eyelets attached high on the wall, so with her gun down, I took my chance. I bounded to grab the rope.

The train's brakes locked with a terrible screeching, and I, as well as everything in the car, jolted forward. I rolled along the wall with all manner of bags and freight uprooted from their positions and carried forward at the rapid slowing. It seemed everything in the car tumbled unchecked toward the front. When the train stopped, I jumped to my feet with my gun drawn and ready. The casket had careened from the ice blocks with unrestrained momentum and crashed into the front of the car with enough force to break it apart. The lantern that had been resting on top had broken and flames had ignited the dripping kerosene and were climbing up the front wall of the car.

I hurriedly stepped over the heaping pile of previously organized freight to arrest Miss Trudeau for the theft of the gold. With one hand, I moved a couple of casket boards until I could see she lay crumpled against the front of the car. Her neck had obviously been broken in the fall. Her mouth lay agape and her eyes stared out, unseeing, in death. The gold ingot had come to rest at her side and one of her arms draped over the cube as though she was trying to hold it close and protect it from harm.

I leaned to rub my finger over the accumulated dirt on the ingot and realized that whoever had been Miss Trudeau's accomplice had buried it in the ingot room. He would have known that once she asked for the body to be held, the logical place for the ice and casket would be directly under the pulley assembly. "Perfect hiding place," I mumbled to myself. No wonder it couldn't be found.

I shook my head as the growing fire suddenly regained my attention. I replaced my pistol to its holster and jerked my coat away to start slapping at the fire on the wall. Between my slapping, I heard someone banging on the door.

"Open this door. What's going on in there?"

A pile of displaced freight prevented the front door from opening and I didn't have time to clear a path because all my effort was being used to put the fire out.

"There's a fire. Come to the back door."

In seconds, the back door opened and light streamed in, then the conductor in his uniform shrieked and joined me in extinguishing the blaze.

When the last flame died, we stepped back to the cleaner, less smoky air. He eyed me up and down, pausing at the badge on my chest. He grunted and pointed to the floor.

"What happened?"

I looked at Miss Trudeau and the gold tucked under her lifeless arm. I permitted myself a deep breath, embarrassed at my unwitting assistance. She had skillfully used every trick, and I had blindly stumbled over myself like an eager-to-please schoolboy.

"They stole a three hundred pound gold ingot from the smelter and tried to sneak it out in a dead man's coffin." I pointed to the front of the car and the broken casket boards scattered there.

"So you killed her?"

I jerked my head at the question. I suppose in a roundabout way she had met her demise because of me, but that hadn't been my intention. "No. She had a gun on me so I pulled the emergency brake. She obviously fell and the heavy coffin and gold hit her hard enough to break her neck."

He nodded. "Well, you sure caused a kerfuffle by locking those brakes." He motioned toward the passenger cars. "Sent me and half the passengers rolling through the cars." He held his arm up to show me blood staining the cuff of his shirt.

I clucked my tongue. "I'm mighty sorry about that. Is anyone else hurt?"

"Mostly bumps and bruises and a few scrapes. Nothing bad that I saw. At least nothing that needs a doc."

"I'm glad to hear that."

He clucked his tongue then stepped toward the open door at the back of the car. Before leaving, he paused and turned. "What are you going to do about her?"

I turned to Miss Trudeau and stared at her with a shake of my head. I felt betrayed and used, but I couldn't bring myself to hate her. I had enjoyed her company and my feelings for her had been genuine. My shoulders sagged and I let out a sigh of regret. I was sorry she was dead. My thoughts turned to the night in the hotel restaurant where she had held my hands. Looking at her on the floor, I felt empty, alone, and most of all, disappointed. How could a girl who seemed so innocent do what she did? If things had been different, she was the kind of girl I could have loved. I stepped closer to gently close her eyes and mouth before climbing over the clutter to the back door of the car. I would have liked to sit with her a little longer, but there was too much to do and too little time to do it. I chanced one more glance to the front of the car and remembered another woman I'd been drawn to. Her name was Molly and I thought at the time I'd been in love with her also. I shook my head. When would I learn?

I turned to the door. I could try to sort

through my feelings later. I leaned out, looking back along the tracks before turning my attention to the conductor who stood at the side. The best solution was for the train to return to Benson where I could notify the Sheriff's Office of Miss Trudeau's death, and I needed to get the ingot back to the smelter. I knew that suggestion wouldn't be taken too kindly by any clock-watching railroad man, but it was a request, no, a demand I had to make. Besides, by my estimate we were only three or four miles from town.

"We need to take the train back to Benson."

A frown was expected and he didn't disappoint me.

"Out of the question. We are already behind schedule."

"I'm afraid I must insist." I tapped my badge." Another half hour won't make that much of a difference."

He started to argue but stopped at a shake of my head. With a barely audible grumble, he left the car and hopped from the platform to the dirt. He looked up one last time, then turned and marched toward the front of the train.

In a few minutes, I saw him walking along the side of the tracks, pointing toward Benson while encouraging the passengers to climb back into the cars. Occasionally, one complained but the conductor simply shrugged and motioned for them to board the train. When he reached me, he stopped and glanced back to make sure the last of the straggling passengers had stepped aboard. He turned to me with a frown.

"We're going back but the engineer is no happier about it that I am. He said he insists you tell the station master why we returned."

"I can do that."

He pointed toward the passenger car with his nose. "Then I suggest you climb aboard."

Chapter 13

As soon as the train came to a stop in Benson, I stepped to the platform. A crowd of onlookers milled about, I was sure wondering why the train had returned. Among them was the deputy. He saw me and marched directly to where I stood.

"What is tarnation is going on here, and where is my horse?" He flailed his arms and clinched his fists. He looked like he wanted to fight.

After learning what I'd learned from Miss Trudeau, I had it in my mind that a no-holds-barred fight might be exactly what I needed. There was nothing like a good knuckle bruising brawl to get a body's mind away from feeling the way I felt. She'd made the fool out of me and it might be good to have some sense knocked back into my brain. But I shook my head and stepped back with hands in front, palms out. "Hold on there, Deputy. You might want to take a look at this before you get too excited." I turned and pointed toward the baggage car.

He lowered his hands. "What is it?"

I released the hasp of the loading door and pushed it open. The freight lay in complete disarray. We stepped over most of it until we stood nearer the front. His eyes opened wide when he saw her there. He looked at me with a questioning expression.

I took a deep breath and pointed to the ingot under her arm. "She stole the gold and tried to get it out in the casket. It was only after the train pulled out that I realized the gold was there."

He cocked his head. "So you killed her?"

I frowned at being asked that question again. She was the last person I'd ever want to harm. "No, I didn't kill her. At least not on purpose. When I pulled the emergency brake, everything in the car shot forward, the gold and casket on the ice the fastest of all. When all that weight hit her, it broke her neck." I turned to him. "A death on the train is in your jurisdiction. I'm reporting it to you."

One of the dock porters peeked into the car and shook his head at the mess. I beckoned him inside and pointed to the gold ingot. "Would you men be so kind as to take that gold and put it in the back of that buggy?" I pointed to the other side of the dock.

"Yessir." He took a step back and looked up the siding, then, with two fingers in his mouth, whistled.

In no time he was joined by three other

porters. The deputy and I stood toward the back of the car and watched them slide the ingot onto one of the casket boards and heft it with a man on each corner. Slowly stepping over the accumulated freight, they made their way to the dock and eventually to the back of the buggy I'd rented from the livery.

The springs creaked under the weight when they allowed the ingot to slide from the board to the buggy floor. I thought for a moment that the panels might break, but they held and I was relieved. I met the porters as they climbed the steps.

"Thank you, men." I gestured to the deputy. "Now, I suspect the deputy here would like some help with a body."

They looked from me to him, then in single file followed him back to the baggage car. Out a sense of duty, or possibly simply because I'd had feelings for her, I watched them indelicately carry Miss Trudeau from the car and place the lifeless body on a shaded bench in front of one of the ticket windows. I felt deep remorse that she was dead, but she'd chosen her hand and had played it to the disastrous end. I stepped slowly to the bench and tidied her body, straightening her legs and folding her arms over her chest. With a final sigh, I brushed her hair from her forehead, then turned away, fighting the urge to remain and stare at her while wishing things had been different.

I rubbed the mare's forehead then stepped into the buggy and turned her toward the smelter. My first order of business was to return the gold, then, if it was the last thing I did, I'd find the woman's accomplice and see him punished for the cold-hearted murder of a man simply because he weighed the same as an ingot of gold.

The pleasant clip-clopping lulled me into a thoughtful state. I let my mind wander over the facts I'd learned about the workings of the smelter and the men there. Because I'd looked through his files, I had already ruled out the head man, Mr. Marks, of any wrongdoing, and I had no reason to suspect Livingston because he'd been honest and forthright to me in every way since my arrival. Other than those two men, everyone else was a suspect.

I thought it best that the first person I should tell about the recovered ingot was Mr. Marks because he was the one who'd formally requested I stay and investigate. He could then send for Livingston and tell him the news.

The mare dropped her head in contented relaxation as I pulled her to a stop in front of the main offices of the smelter company. I looped the lines around the railing at the front of the buggy then jumped down and strode directly through the door to the closest of the clerks.

He glanced up. "Yes, sir?"

"I need to see Mr. Marks."

He looked over his shoulder to the back of the huge room, then returned his attention to me. "I'm afraid he's very busy. Would you care to come back later?"

I looked to the back and saw Marks standing alone at the back windows of the office building. He didn't look busy. I turned to the clerk, clinching my teeth in frustration. I was in no mood to be told the man was too busy to see me. "This is important. He'll want to see me."

The clerk nervously glanced toward the back one more time, although I didn't know which of us he feared more. Finally, with a sigh and an apprehensive swallow, he beckoned me follow him. As we approached, Marks turned. His face was pale and he appeared tired and unwell. He nodded weakly then pointed to a chair opposite his desk before plopping into his own.

The clerk quickly disappeared. I took the offered seat and held my hat in my hands.

"Good morning Marshal." His voice was lifeless and distant. "It's a nasty business to have to send a dead man to the train. I wanted to tell Miss Trudeau one last time of our sadness, but I couldn't get away. Two men from the investor group showed up today and relieved me of my duties because of the lost ingot." He waved his arm." I've been here from the beginning, but I've been dismissed. The only reason I'm here now is to clean out my desk." He absently studied his fingers as they rubbed the shiny mahogany.

The chair creaked as I sat up. "But Mr. Marks, that's what I wanted to see you about. I've found the ingot. The reason for my visit is to return it to you."

His head snapped up. "You found it?"

I pointed over my shoulder with my thumb. "It's in the buggy."

He stood with instantly renewed strength and bolted around the desk and into the aisle leading to the front door. I hurried to follow him, but didn't catch up until we both leaned on the buggy wheels to look inside. I reached to lift a cloth I'd used to cover the ingot from any inquisitive folks that might decide they wanted it more than me.

Marks extended his hand to caress the smooth gold. He didn't speak for a full minute. Finally, he glanced up. "Where was it?"

"In the casket."

He leaned back suddenly. "In the casket? How in the world did it end up there?"

I told the story of Miss Trudeau and how she and an accomplice had set the plan into motion, how she had played us all for fools and how they'd been able to get a three hundred pound block of mostly pure gold out of the ingot room with no one the wiser.

He rubbed his forehead. "But she seemed so sweet and innocent."

He was right about that. Her play-acting had been superb and I had fallen hardest of all. I tapped the wheel of the buggy. "She certainly seemed that way."

He glanced up. "And where is she now?"

I frowned as I remembered her pushed against the front of the freight car. "Dead."

He shook his head as if trying to rattle his brain to understand the word. "Dead? Did you kill her?"

There was that question again. Why did everyone assume I had killed her? "No. she died of an accidental fall, but before she died, she admitted to stealing the ingot."

He immediately stiffened. "She couldn't have done it alone."

I pursed my lips and nodded. "That's the other reason I'm here to see you today. How did you know to contact her in Santa Fe after Peter's death?"

His face screwed up in concentration then he opened his eyes wide. "From his file. We have all employees list a person we should contact if an emergency arises."

"Who keeps the files?"

"Livingston."

I coughed and suddenly couldn't catch my breath. I'd trusted Livingston just as I had trusted Miss Trudeau. How could I have been so blind? And not only once, but twice, and my trusting was coming back to haunt me again. If Livingston was the keeper of the files, it would have been an easy task to change the name and address of the emergency contact.

It all made perfect sense now. Livingston was one of only two men with a key to the ingot room and one of only a handful of men authorized to be there without supervision. He, like Miss Trudeau, had played his part well, appearing so concerned with any entry into the ingot room.

He'd had Peter's body placed under the block and tackle, according to him, to make it easier to move the weight, but I could see the real reason now. It made it easy to place a gold ingot into the casket so I could escort Miss Trudeau to the train station. I thought of the show he'd made about leaving her alone in the ingot room, then he hurried to his office to get some work done. I frowned and shook my head. He had obviously hurried around the side and through the smelter to help her get rid of Peter's body and load the gold into its place. And to top that, he'd been the one who had supplied the small nails to me. He had watched me nail the coffin shut, all the time knowing that it would be simple to open it and make the switch.

I looked to Marks. "I think we need to have a word with Mr. Livingston."

He frowned. "I'm sure Livingston was not involved. I trust him completely."

I clucked my tongue. "I trusted him also, but

think about it. He had the files and could easily have changed the name of who to contact. He had free run of the smelter and the ingot room and he was Peter's boss. Who better to sneak up behind and kill him with a blow to the head?"

Marks slowly breathed in and out, then his eyes opened wide. "But he's not big enough to have moved Peter's body to the pour floor."

"That's true if Peter was killed at a different place in the smelter, but he could easily have instructed his subordinate to accompany him there so he could kill him when no one was looking." I waved a hand over my shoulder toward the smelter. "You've been on the pour floor. It's hidden from the view of almost everyone except Huish and Collins when they stand on their platform. I've already discovered that they are away from that station much more than they like to admit." I rubbed my face. "I'm not positive Livingston's guilty, but he has some explaining to do."

The portly man dropped his head in sad agreement. "Very well. Let's go to his desk."

After replacing the cloth, we entered the building. He led while I followed through the maze of desks to the back. Livingston was nowhere to be seen.

Marks leaned to the closest desk-man. "James, Where's Livingston?"

The man glanced toward me then back to Marks with a shrug. "He left a couple of hours ago. Said he had some business in town."

I clinched my teeth. Of course he would be gone. He thought the gold was away and on the train heading north. Why would he stay? He was probably making arrangements to go to Santa Fe to divide the spoils with his beautiful accomplice.

I turned to Marks. "Do you need any more proof than that?"

A deep breath was my answer.

The filing cabinets under the windows along the back wall caught my attention. I pointed. "Are those the files you spoke of?"

Marks nodded.

"Can you find Peter's?"

He turned to James. "Peter Trudeau's file please."

James jumped and hurried to the cabinet. In only a few seconds, he pulled what looked like a large envelope, which he passed over. Marks motioned for me to join him at Livingston's desk. We leaned over as he opened the envelope and pulled papers from inside. He shuffled through several then pulled one and set it to the side. With his finger, he traced down the page, finally stopping and tapping.

"Right here. Trudy Trudeau. Chisolm House. Santa Fe, New Mexico Territory."

I leaned over the desk and followed his finger as he read, but something was amiss. I leaned closer and pointed to the writing. "Who writes these out?"

He frowned and cocked his head. "The worker being hired unless he can't write, then Livingston or one of his men do it. Why?"

I scratched at the writing at the top of the page with a blunt fingernail. The penmanship was blocky, heavily written with no attempt at flair. It was likely Peter's writing. I moved to the section Marks had read. The contrast was obvious and I blinked. The facts in my brain rattled around the assumption I'd made that Livingston was the culprit, but that possibility vanished with sudden understanding. I knew who the accomplice was, and it wasn't Livingston.

The relief I felt made my head drop and I breathed with a nod. I tapped the top of the paper again. "Look at this writing. Would you agree that it is surely Peter's?"

He leaned in. "I think that is a reasonable conclusion."

I moved my hand down. "Then take a gander at how luxurious the writing is here. It was certainly written by a different hand that Peter's."

"Yes. I can see that. But you said yourself that Livingston would have changed the name and address of the person to contact in the event of an emergency."

"That I did." I rummaged around Livingston's desk. When I found a sheaf of papers he'd been working on, I flipped several pages and smiled inwardly at what I saw.

"Look at this." I pushed the papers closer to Marks.

"What am I supposed to look at?"

"Compare Livingston's writing to the flowing penmanship for the emergency contact. Could Livingston have written that?"

He shook his head, then immediately brightened. "Absolutely not. That means Livingston is not the accomplice."

I nodded.

His eyebrows pulled down. "Then who is?"

I turned to James who stood warily watching us from ten feet away. "Would you please find the file for Jonas Collins?"

"Yes sir." He stepped briskly to one of the

cabinets and searched from the front to the back. He turned with a grunt. "It's not here."

Of course it wasn't there. Collins was smart. He must have removed it to prevent us from comparing the penmanship on Peter's emergency contact paper. I tapped my foot then had an idea. "Then find me one of these files that would have been written by Collins when he was working for Livingston while recuperating from his accident."

He opened a different file and shuffled through several before pulling one and handing it to me. On the front of the envelope in bold script was the name, GONZALES, LUPE C. I opened it, glancing quickly at the papers before slapping the papers on the desk in front of Marks. I leaned back smugly and snapped the lapels of my coat.

"You tell me."

A low whistle escaped his lips. "How did you know?"

"Something Livingston told me the other day. I'd asked about Collins and he mentioned how he worked here during his recovery. He said the man was not a good bookkeeper but his penmanship was of the highest quality."

Marks chewed on a thumbnail. "And in his position he has full run of the smelter and ingot room."

"Exactly."

Without putting the papers back into the envelope, I passed the bundle to James to return to the cabinet. I motioned for Marks to lead the way back to the buggy and the gold. We needed to get that back to the ingot room before it disappeared again.

As we reached the door, we happily greeted

Livingston at his return from town. Marks reached and vigorously shook his hand.

"Great to see you Livingston. Come take a peek at what Hawk showed up with." He walked directly to the buggy and flipped the cloth away from the ingot.

Livingston's eyes grew wide and the surprised relief on his face was plain for all to see. He turned to me. "Where was it?"

I pointed toward the river bridge and told the story again, this time making sure it was clear that I did not kill Miss Trudeau. I also added that my suspect for her accomplice was Collins. The only thing I kept to myself was our initial suspicion that Livingston was somehow involved. That could come later.

He shook his head. "So the switch for Peter's body must have been made while she was alone in the ingot room."

"Had to be. I checked the casket before I nailed it shut, and other than the time she was alone with it and the time we sat in the buggy waiting for the freight wagon, it didn't leave my sight until it was loaded and the train left."

He breathed deeply. "Then Peter's body is somewhere in the ingot room." He pointed toward the back then tapped the side rail of the buggy. "Let's get the ingot back where it belongs, then I think we owe it to Peter to find him and give him a proper burial."

Marks clapped my back. "Thanks for bringing it back. I'm heading to town to see the investors and let them know. Maybe I can keep my job." He turned back into the building.

The springs creaked when Livingston and I

climbed into the buggy. I coaxed the mare into a trot and made a wide-circle turn to the wood yard and down to the ingot room. I waited while Livingston opened the door, then I drove in and stopped directly under the block and tackle.

Livingston lit a lantern and set it on the ground, then worked the ropes to let the pulleys down. The buggy raised as the block and tackle took the weight of the gold and it seemed to me that the springs sighed in relief. Livingston let the rope slide though his hands until the ingot settled into the mud left over from the ice under Peter's casket.

We unhooked the pulleys and tied them to the wall where they belonged. I stood under them with arms folded in the coolness of the room. Now that the ingot was in its place, I was anxious to arrest Collins, although I suspected he had pulled out when the gold left the property. He had a good head start but I had an advantage. He wouldn't know that the ingot had been returned or that Miss Trudeau was dead. And most of all, he wouldn't know I was on his trail.

Livingston raised his nose in the air. "Do you smell that?"

I sniffed but caught no trace of any odor other than the dank smell of the cave-like room. "I can't smell anything."

He didn't answer but held the lantern high and started walking along the wall at the back of the room. He pulled a metal pin from a hasp and let it hang by a small chain, then pulled opened a wooden door to a good-sized room against the back wall. The dim light from the lantern seemed reluctant to penetrate the darkness and the room was black as night inside. I got an ominous feeling, but, against my better judgement, I followed Livingston to the center of the room where Peter's corpse lay face down on the dirt. The smell burned my nose and I stepped back in hopes of getting a breath of fresher air.

Without warning, the door slammed and I heard the unmistakable sound of the pin dropping into the hasp, then retreating footsteps as whoever was there ran away.

Chapter 14

A sinking feeling pressed on my chest. I rushed to the door to push against it, but there was no give. It was solidly built and I could tell from my pounding that the boards were thick and unbreakable.

I looked to Livingston as he approached with the lantern.

"Is there another door?"

He swallowed hard and shook his head. "This room was originally built to store the silver and gold ingots until we realized that storing them directly under the cooling floor would save a lot of work. It hasn't been used in years, but it was designed to be almost impenetrable."

I pressed my face against the door to look through the slits between the boards. I saw the light coming through the big door and the silhouette of the man who'd locked us in. He disappeared from sight for a moment then I saw him running toward the buggy while holding the pulleys to keep them from swinging. I watched in amazement as he expertly hooked the ingot and used the block and tackle to load it into the buggy.

I looked at Livingston, who also had his face against the boards.

"He loaded the ingot back into my buggy!"

Livingston kicked the wood.

I gazed out in hopeless frustration. We had unwittingly given the man an unprecedented opportunity and he was taking full advantage of it. He unhooked the pulleys then climbed into the buggy and started the mare into a tight turn to leave through the door to the outside. The last thing I saw was the big door slowly rolling shut, bringing increasing darkness to the room.

I stepped back. "The guards. You said they are stationed at the gate to the wood yard and search every wagon. Surely they'll stop him and search the buggy. He won't be able to get away."

He frowned. "The guards are only there when I schedule them to be there. I know when a wagon is going in so I tell them when to man their post. There is no one there to notice the buggy."

I grunted at his explanation and clenched my teeth, hissing my words. "There's got to be a way out. If we don't stop him, he'll get away with almost a hundred thousand in gold." I peeked one last time through the space then slapped the thick plank. "Damn!"

We had only one lantern so we worked our way together along the walls, running our hands over the thick, rough-cut lumber. The slits between the boards gave me initial hope but none were wide enough to slip more than my finger through. We examined the rock wall at the back and found the mortar between the stones to be tight and thick. Not even a sliver of light could be seen through the cracks.

High on the wall, approximately ten feet from the ground, two small openings allowed a tiny amount of light into the room, but even without closer inspection, I could see they were much too small for either of us to fit through. My gaze continued upward as Livingston held the lantern high. I could see the slats and adobe of the ceiling ten feet above our heads, but nothing I saw gave me any hope.

I breathed a sigh of distress. "Any ideas?"

Livingston licked his lips while shaking his head.

"There's got to be a way to get the door open." I pointed and motioned for him to join me there.

He held the lantern while I ran my fingers over every inch of the door. The thick planks were sturdily nailed to the cross braces and only a thin space was visible between the boards, except for one knothole low to the ground. I lay on the dirt and pushed my arm through, but all I felt was open air and my arm was much too short to disengage the pin from the hasp. Disgusted, I stood, then kicked in vain at the edge of the door hoping to dislodge the hasp, but the kicking did little more than make my foot hurt.

I hobbled back and stood with my thumbs

tucked into my belt when I noticed Livingston scrape the dirt floor with his boot then drop to his knees. My eyes opened wide and I joined him, but it was immediately obvious that the dirt was too dry and too packed for us to dig with our hands. I sat on my heels with my fists on my hips. If only we had some type of implement.

I glanced around then reached for the lantern to search for something, anything, but a quick trip through the room turned up nothing useful. I returned to the door where Livingston sat dejectedly with his back against the boards.

The air in the room grew colder as I knelt close to him. I held my hands over the lantern chimney and rubbed them together then folded my arms.

"Let's take stock. What do we have of use?" I tapped my gun then counted silently as I ran my fingers over the cartridge loops on my belt. "I have a pistol and fifteen rounds of ammunition. If I shoot through the hole, will anyone in the smelter hear and come to investigate?"

He stared at the hole in the door. "Too noisy in the smelter. They'd never hear it." He tapped the planks. "Do you think you can shoot through the boards?"

I leaned to the knothole and placed the fingers of my hand on each side. The boards were at least two inches thick. I made a face. "I doubt it but it's worth a try. Stand back."

The shot was loud in the confines of the room. I re-holstered my pistol then held the lantern close, hoping for more, but not surprised that the bullet had penetrated less than an inch. I shook my head. "We'll never be able to shoot our way out of here."

He frowned then slid his hand into his suit

coat pocket. "I have three pencils." He held them so I could see.

I didn't know how three pencils could help, but it was a start. "What else?"

"My pocket watch." He pulled it out and flipped the cover. "It's a quarter to four."

I brightened. "The office workers will be heading home in the next couple of hours. Any chance they will notice anything amiss and come to investigate?"

He sighed. "Possible but not likely. Other than Marks, the others don't seem to notice what goes on back here."

"And Marks has already gone for the day."

"Unfortunately, yes."

I impatiently pulled my coat closer around me to ward off the increasing cold. I was thankful that I had a heavier coat. Livingston had only a checkered business coat and his intermittent shivering told how little warmth it held.

He grunted and reached into his pocket. "I almost forgot about this." He held up a small, folding knife and handed it to me.

The blade was tiny, less than two inches and I frowned as I ran my finger along the marginally sharp edge. I glanced at Livingston and my frustration must have shown on my face.

"Sorry. I only use it to open envelopes." He pocketed the knife when I handed it back.

I felt my pockets. I generally carried a jack knife but had broken it and had not yet gotten a replacement. Something in the back of my mind tickled my consciousness. I closed my eyes and rubbed my temples with my fingers. Something was there but I couldn't quite bring it to the front. It had something to do with the smelter building, but what could it be? My eyes snapped open. Of course!

"Livingston, do you remember when you told me that the Mexican boy lives in a shack on the other side of the wall?"

"Juan?" Yes, he does. Not more than fifty yards away."

I reached for his hand to help him to his feet, then we walked to the other side of the room. "I'll kneel down. If you'll stand on my shoulders, I'll lift you up. You should be high enough to see out."

He took off his boots, then with hands against the stone wall, stood on my shoulders. I slowly rose to my feet.

"I can see it." The excitement in his voice was contagious.

"Anyone there?"

"No. But let me see if I can get some attention." He pressed his face into the hole and whistled loudly, then waited a quarter minute before whistling again.

He waited for what seemed a long time, but no response came from the shack. He slapped the wall. "Nobody over there. Let me down so you can rest then we'll try it again in a few minutes."

We repeated our attempt every fifteen minutes until the day's light was gone, then we retreated to the door and sat on the dirt. I crossed my ankles and reached for the lantern. I shook it gently to hear the kerosene slosh inside and realized that we had only a few hours of the fuel remaining. I cupped my hand over the chimney and blew out the flame. Instant darkness pressed around us, and with it, a feeling of hopelessness.

It was going to be a long night. I unbuckled my

gun belt and placed it on the ground then I leaned and settled to the dirt with my coat pulled close to conserve what heat I could. "We might as well try to get some sleep. At first light we'll try to raise someone at the shack."

Sleep would not come in the cold of the night. I thought of the man who'd locked us in the room. Had it been Collins? Judging from the expert way he'd handled the block and tackle I was almost certain it had been him. I shook my head. If I had been in his boots, I would have left the smelter the minute the train departed. If the gold was away, what reason could he have had to stay unless it was to keep any suspicion directed to someone else and away from him. That was logical, I supposed, but that would have meant he had absolute trust in Miss Trudeau.

I suddenly remembered a conversation I'd had with the deputy in town. He'd mentioned that Collins hadn't been interested in any of the local girls because he had a lover up north. Could that have been Miss Trudeau? And if they were in this together, were they alone? I couldn't fathom that they would bring someone else into the scheme. Why would they? The more people who knew about the murder and theft, the greater the chance of discovery.

Too many questions and not enough answers, but the one answer I did have was that I needed to get out of the room and get the gold back.

The cold pressed on us with a suffocating weight, and I never knew how long a single night could be. And never was such a small amount of light through two small openings more welcome than it was when the gray light of dawn could be seen after the insufferable night.

We lit the lantern and set it on the dirt, then standing on my shoulders, Livingston whistled through the opening. He got no response so I lowered him to the ground.

He sat on the floor to pull on his boots, then stood and slapped his hands on his upper arms in an attempt at warmth. "I can see smoke from the chimney so I know they are there. They go out for wood every day, we only need to catch them while they are outside."

I rubbed my shoulders and took a deep breath. I didn't want to tell Livingston, but I hadn't eaten since breakfast the day before and I could feel my strength waning. I guessed he was in the same condition. If we didn't get out soon, we would be in real trouble.

Five minutes later I lifted him so he could look through the opening again. "I see them!" He whistled long and loud and waited. He grunted and whistled again then yelled through the opening. "Juan. Juan, help us."

He paused for a few seconds before screaming again. "Juan, don't leave. Over here. Help us." Seconds later his voice lowered and he sounded close to tears. "They can't hear me."

I reached for my pistol, forgetting that I'd taken my belt off the night before. "Jump down, Livingston. I'll get my gun."

I dropped to my knees then he jumped to the dirt and ran to my holster and back. I stood, bracing myself against the wall with him on my shoulders. I heard three shots in rapid succession, then another three, then the impatient, futile clicking of the hammer against already spent shells.

I suspected the answer but asked anyway. "Anything?" I lowered him until he could jump down, and when I saw his face I knew they hadn't heard.

He shook his head and his breath caught in his throat and fear showed on his face. "They've crossed over the hill. There is no way they can hear us now. They were our last hope."

"Livingston, pull yourself together." I reached and grasped his shoulders. "We'll just have to think of something else."

He sank to the ground and leaned against the rock wall. His shoulders sagged as he stared, blank-faced, across the room. "We're going to die here."

"No we aren't. Not if I can do anything about it. Let's take stock again. What do you have besides three pencils and the toy knife?"

He reached into his pockets and laid the contents on the floor between us. Three pencils, the knife, a small box of matches for the lantern, two silver dollars and a button. He looked up and shrugged.

From my pockets I pulled four quarters, a nickel, my pocket watch and a handkerchief, then brought my gun belt from the other side of the room. He handed me the pistol, which I slid into the holster, then kneeled and placed it on the ground. I looked at the pile then at his panic-stricken face. "Don't give up yet." I reached for the matches. They rattled inside the box when I shook it. I looked at the pencils, then the lantern.

"Are you willing to take a chance?"

His eyes blinked heavily but he didn't answer. I grabbed his arm and shook him.

"Will the smelter be fully staffed this

morning?"

He shook the cobwebs from his brain. "This morning?"

"Yes. Will all the workers be on duty?"

He rubbed his jaw. "What's today?"

"Friday."

"Yes, everyone should be there, why?"

I shook the matches again. "It's time for drastic measures." I pointed in the direction of the smelter. "Do you think a fire will bring the workers running?"

He looked to the ceiling. "Maybe, but we don't have anything to burn and they wouldn't see a fire inside this room."

I stood and pulled him to his feet. "They will see the wall burning."

His eyes opened wide. "There's nowhere for the smoke to go. It will kill us."

"Maybe so, but I think not." I pointed to the corner away from the door. "We can start the fire there, then lay low on the opposite corner with our coats over us. With any luck, the workers will see the fire and get us out before we suffocate."

He shook his head. "And without any luck?"

I didn't answer but waited for him to make his decision. Finally, he nodded. "All right, let's give it a try."

I retrieved my quarters and nickel, buckled my gun belt and shoved the handkerchief and watch back into my pocket, then picked up the pencils and the lantern.

I led the way to the far corner then kneeled and opened his small knife. With it, I shaved long splinters from the pencils, then opened the cap to the kerosene reservoir in the lantern. I slid the slivers in and held them one by one until each was saturated, then I pushed them through the widest gap between the thick boards.

"I'm going to try to get most of the fire started on the outside rather than the inside. That way we might have more time before the smoke overtakes us."

He nodded while nervously rubbing his temples. The first match lit with a loud pop. I held it through the gap under the pencil slivers and within seconds, a small flame could be seen. The larger it got, the faster it spread until the entire bundle of kindling was aflame and the fire licked at the boards of the wall. We retreated to the opposite corner and sat there, watching and waiting.

More quickly than I expected, the fire spread to the adjacent boards and climbed rapidly. Smoke boiled to the ceiling and in the light of the fire, I could see it gathering, cloudlike, hugging the slat and adobe ceiling. With each minute, it grew thicker and lower. I looked at Livingston. He nodded with determination then lowered himself to the floor and covered his head with his coat. I glanced once again to the growing fire and did the same.

I closed my eyes tightly and breathed in shallow, controlled breaths through the handkerchief and coat. Before long the smoke became increasingly pungent and I heard Livingston coughing. I peeked over my coat and saw the entire corner of the room in mighty blaze. The smoke burned my eyes so I squeezed them tight and pulled my coat closer, all the while hoping the men would come soon.

Livingston's coughing grew more severe and I fought the urge with each breath until I could control it no longer. The fire roared with surprising intensity, much louder than I had imagined. I knew we were safe from the fire and that the danger came exclusively from the smoke, which grew thicker and hotter by the second. We both coughed in unrelenting spasms and I cursed myself for thinking up the hair-brained plan in the first place.

I'd given up hope. The men hadn't come and our time had run out. I rolled to my knees and coughed in hacking, painful contractions. My lungs felt like the fire had invaded them and I was burning from the inside out.

I felt myself being lifted from the floor. I'd always wondered what death was like and if I'd be lifted and carried heavenward. The air suddenly became pure and I breathed in, tasting the exquisite atmosphere of the hereafter. I could hear commotion around me and wondered if the angels were making preparations to do whatever they did. Then, I felt and heard nothing.

Chapter 15

The dull pain in the back of my head intensified as I slowly attempted to open one eye. The pain wasn't worth it so I gave up and held both closed in a squint. From somewhere I heard a dull, faint voice, it sounded like someone was trying to sing and doing a terrible job of it. I was sure it was no angel. I breathed deeply and the resulting cough made my head feel like it would explode. I rolled to my side and placed my hand over my brow, rubbing to relieve some of the pain.

The singing stopped and I soon felt a hand on my shoulder. "Welcome back, Mr. Hawk."

Using my hand as shade from the harsh light, I rolled to my back and opened one eye to look into a round, whiskery face and yellow-toothed grin. I didn't recognize the man so I rubbed both eyes and looked again, but with the same conclusion.

"Who are you?"

The man snickered and tapped his chest. "I'm Doc Marlee."

I searched my brain for any recollection of the man, but came up empty. "Where am I?"

He snickered again. "Why, you're in what the smelter company calls the infirmary. They keep this room for anyone who gets sick or hurt on the job."

At the mention of the smelter, the memory of the inferno came rushing back and a sudden urge to cough could not be denied. When finished, I knew I was obviously alive because if I was dead, my body could not hurt so badly.

After another coughing fit and several minutes rest, I looked up to see Doc Marlee standing over me again. I rubbed my temples and moved my head from side to side trying to work some of the stiffness out. I moved my arms, then my legs, happy to see them responding, but surprised at how sore I was from the top of my head to the soles of my feet.

I noticed I was under a single, cotton sheet and was naked from the top of my head to the bottoms of my feet. I frowned and tried to sit up, but he pushed me down.

"Hold on there young feller. You've been through a hard time. You need to rest so you can get well."

My head settled back into the pillow and I relaxed. "How long have I been here?"

He reached and pulled my eyelids back one at a time and studied my eyes, then tapped my chest and listened with a contraption stuck into his ears.

When finished he placed the listening device around his neck and grunted while shaking his head. "Two days."

"Two days? I've been here two days? I've got things to do."

I attempted to rise again but he held my shoulders to the bed.

"You can get up, but you'll have to move slow." He reached and took my arm. Now, sit up careful like."

With his help, I was able to sit, but the room started spinning and I thought I would black out. He held my arm until the dizziness passed, then he allowed me to swing my legs to the side of the bed.

He stepped back. "Now you rest there for a bit. If you try to stand I'll have to pick you up from the floor."

I took his advice and placed my hands to my side, held to the mattress and tried to breathe. I tilted my head left and right then turned to see each direction. The bed next to mine was occupied and I was happy to see Livingston asleep there. I hadn't noticed him.

I waved my arm. "How's Livingston?"

Doc Marlee glanced toward my friend. "He's weak, but I'm confident he'll be waking up soon. Neither of you were physically burned, but you each took in a lot of smoke. Only time will tell how much damage was done, but you're both young and if things go well, I don't foresee any long-term problems."

I nodded, hoping that was the case.

He brought a bundle of clothes and placed them on the bed. I recognized them as mine. He smiled at my unasked question.

"Smoke through all your clothes stunk to high heaven. Marks had everything sent to the Chinese laundry on the other side of town. You can get dressed if you like."

I pulled the bow of the tie string and lifted out my long-handles. I was able to get them on my legs and over my shoulders but the effort was exhausting. I felt as though I would faint so I rested on the bed for a long time.

The doc strolled to my side and pointed over his shoulder. "I've got some fried beef and bread on the table yonder. Care for any?"

I was weak and my head ached, but my stomach growled at the mention of food. "I'd be obliged."

He helped me stand, then with my arm over his shoulder and his arm around my waist, we made it to the table where I sat and leaned on my elbows. He pushed a full plate toward me along with a pitcher and a glass. I looked at the glass but grabbed the pitcher and drank at least half the water directly from it. It was the best tasting water I'd ever had the privilege to swallow. The cold beef and bread was likewise among the best I'd ever had.

After finishing, I wiped my mouth with the sleeve of my long-handles and leaned back before turning in the chair to observe the doc listening to Livingston's chest. He stood and nodded.

I returned the nod then tapped the table. "Thanks for the grub. Best I've ever had."

He smiled then patted his oversized belly. "My wife's cooking. It'll grow on you." He cackled and slapped his hip.

I chuckled weakly and scooted my chair so I could face him. I could feel some strength returning after the meal, and hard as it was, I realized the best course was for me to take it easy for a while. Unfortunately, every day I spent recuperating was a day Collins was farther away with the gold.

I impatiently tapped my foot. "How soon until I can leave?"

The doc cocked his head. "A couple of days, minimum. Three would be better."

I thought about it. Two days was far too long and three days was out of the question. I drummed my fingers on the table while I planned my moves. I wanted to talk to the liveryman to see if the mare and buggy had been seen in town, and if so, was Collins the driver? I also wanted to spend some time with the deputy to learn what he knew about my suspect and where he might have gone. I could question both men while taking it easy, then as soon as I felt up to it, I would be on my way to track Collins down. It was a matter of pride as well as revenge. No one was going to try to kill me while stealing almost a hundred thousand dollars in gold and get away with it.

I rose slowly and hobbled back to my bed to sit on the edge and look at the doc. "What's today?"

"Sunday."

"What time is it?"

The gold pocket watch slipped from his vest when he pulled the chain. He held it in the palm of his fat hand and studied it. He glanced up. "Pert near six o'clock."

"Morning or evening?"

"Evening." The watch slipped easily into the pocket, then the doc patted his chest, sides and legs as though he was searching for anything that might have gotten lost in a pocket. Satisfied that there was nothing, he reached and pulled the sheet to Livingston's throat then turned to me.

"Ordinarily I'd be heading home now, but Marks said he'd pay me to stay through the nights as long as either of you were here." He rubbed the stubble on his jaw. "I've been here since Friday when they carried you in."

I reached for my clothes, but he held his hand on my shoulder.

"What do you think you're doing? You can't go out. You need to rest."

The doc stepped closer as I straightened and stood with one hand holding my jeans and the other braced on the bed.

I looked into his face. I knew he was right but my pride wouldn't let me lay around any longer. I was young and strong, and, I recognized, bull headed. "Plenty of time to rest later. I've got things to do." I leaned against the bed for a moment. I was weak, and the thought of how close I'd come to dying didn't add to my strength, but I had a job to do and the longer I waited, the harder the gold would be to find.

I glanced at him, determined that I wouldn't let him stop me. I'd been hurt worse and had gotten by fine. I pushed away from the bed and leaned with my pants, but I suddenly got light headed. I could see him waiting with arms folded and a smug grin. When the moment passed, I pushed away from the bed for the second time and leaned to get one foot into the garment. Suddenly weak, I fell against the doc. He held me with strong arms and guided me back to the bed."

The bed creaked as he allowed me to sit. I looked up. "I've got places I need to__." That was the last thing I remembered.

The single sheet rested under my chin as I opened my eyes. The room was dark, with a single lantern on the same table I'd eaten on earlier, and when I lifted my head, I could see the doc sitting and reading next to the light. Livingston's outline was visible on the bed next to me. Soft snores came from him, which I took to be a good sign. I threw the sheet back, rolled to my side and carefully pushed to sit on the edge of my bed.

The doc got up and strolled to my side. "Good morning."

I rubbed my face. "Morning?"

He chuckled. "Yep. You slept the whole night through." He pulled his watch. "It's nine o'clock. I suspect you're feeling a mite stronger than you were yesterday."

I rolled my head in a circle to stretch my neck muscles. "I am."

He smiled then pointed to the next bed. "You'll be happy to know that Livingston woke up. He ate and drank then went back to sleep."

My bare feet touched the polished, hardwood floor as I pushed forward and stood. "That's good news." I motioned toward my clothes. "Reckon I could go now? I'd sure like to talk to Mr. Marks."

He gathered my boots, coat and gun belt and carried them to the chair. "Go right ahead. If you'll move slow, you should be all right. In fact, Marks asked me to let him know when you were awake. If you'll promise to stay seated until I get back I'll go to the office building and let one of the men get a message to him."

Arguing the day before had gotten me nowhere so I agreed. "I promise."

He winked with a grin, then left. I reached to pull my boots on one at a time then I stood to swing the gun belt behind and catch it with my left hand. I buckled it and pushed it down, then pulled my coat to my shoulders. I retook the seat and tapped my foot impatiently waiting for the doc to return.

Within minutes he walked through the door and directly to me. He reached a hand and pulled me to my feet. "Remember what I said, you take it slow." He pointed over his shoulder with his thumb. "Marks will be waiting for you."

I followed him to the door where he reached for the handle and pushed outward. The winter sun blazed brightly through the cloudless sky and cool, winter air. I squinted and held my hand in front of my eyes for a full minute until I could look around and get my bearings. I saw the smoke stack and the office building fifty yards away. Marks was expecting me, but I doubted he knew that I bore bad news about the ingot being stolen again. I gritted my teeth. I would get it back and I would bring Collins in to hang for the murder of Peter Trudeau. It was no longer simply a matter of U.S. Marshal work, it was as much my pride that would push me as far as I needed to go.

From the doorjamb where I leaned, I looked down at Doc Marlee. "Thanks, doc."

He cackled then grabbed my hand in both of his. "Didn't do much other than watch you sleep." He got serious. "And you mind what I told you about going slow for a few days."

"I'll do that, thanks." I turned toward the office building in the crisp, morning air and walked slowly on the path. When I stepped through the office building door, the front desk man stood.

He hurried to my side then pointed to the back. "Mr. Marks is anxious to see you, sir."

I frowned, wondering how anxious he would be if he knew the bad news I brought. "Thank you." I strolled past, in and out of the maze of desks, until I got to the door of Marks's office. He wasn't alone, but he turned all his attention to me as soon as he saw me standing there. He stood, as did his visitor who turned to look at me.

I swallowed hard and stared. I needed to sit down. The man who returned my gaze was none other than Collins, the very man I'd sworn to bring in for justice.

Marks hurried around his desk and reached his hand for a shake. "Come in Marshal Hawk. I can't tell you how happy we are that you were unharmed in that unfortunate incident in the ingot room." He pulled me into the room.

I was so stunned I could scarcely move. My feet felt like I was walking through molasses. Marks gently pushed me into a chair facing them both. I swallowed and blinked. None of this was making sense. Why would a murderer and thief be sitting so casually only three feet from me?

Collins's face and reserved smile was the picture of contentment. He leaned his head back and shook his shoulder length hair from his ears before turning to Marks. I also turned my attention to the head man. What else could I do?

Marks leaned forward to place his elbows on the desk and cocked his head with a wry smile. "Marshal Hawk, do you know how you got out of the room during the fire?"

I shook my head. "No, sir."

He motioned toward the long-haired man.

"Collins saw the fire from his perch in the smelter. When he got there, he saw the door pinned on the outside and heard coughing on the inside. He carried both of you out. The doc said if not for him, you would both have died."

I squinted my eyes in thought. How could that be? Collins was the one who locked us there in the first place then loaded the gold into my buggy. It didn't make sense. He'd killed Peter, so obviously death caused him no hesitation. Why would he save Livingston and me?

I studied Marks. He knew of my suspicion, we'd talked of it when I returned the first ingot. Had he shared that information with Collins? I looked from one man to the other, wondering about the big man's presence. I could only guess that he didn't know he was my prime suspect. I slowly pulled my pistol and held it unobtrusively on my lap, but Collins sat unmoving, with arms folded and ankles crossed. I casually held my gun, not directly pointing at him, but ready just in case. I studied him. If he was nervous, he didn't show it.

I cleared my throat then coughed long and hard. My chest burned and I held my hand to my throat. When finished, I wiped my mouth with my sleeve then turned to the man in the chair.

"Mr. Collins, let me tell you something about police work. When a crime is committed, we investigate, and in the course of the investigation, we identify individuals who might have been the perpetrators. As we continue to gather evidence, we grow more convinced of the person's guilt or innocence." I waved my free hand. "Take this case for example. Someone murdered Peter Trudeau. During my search for clues I've had several smelter workers high on my suspect list, but each has been cleared as I've uncovered additional information." I swallowed and squinted. "I have to tell you that you are currently my top suspect. What do you have to say about that?"

The corners of his mouth turned down as he slowly shook his head. He tilted his head toward the third man in the room. "Mr. Marks here called for me just now. Said you needed to talk to me, but I can tell you right here and now that I ain't never killed anybody, especially Peter Trudeau." He uncrossed his feet and sat up in the chair with his hands on the arms. "Whatever gave you the idea that I did?"

I used the barrel of the gun to push my hat back on my head then motioned toward the other side of the office building where Livingston worked. "Your writing."

He frowned and his brushy eyebrows pulled down. "My writing?"

"Yep. You changed the emergency contact information for Peter. It's on the card over in Livingston's office. I've seen it myself."

His hair bobbed around his face when he shook his head, and his eyes, which had been calm until then, intensely bored into me. I remembered my time with him on the perch and my hope at the time that he wouldn't throw me off the tower. I was glad I had my gun out.

He leaned forward in the chair. "I never changed anything on Peter's card. What makes you think I did?"

I peered at the man, using my honed skills to determine if he was lying. "We compared your writing from another file to the writing on Peter's card. It matched perfectly."

He slapped the arms of the chair and my hold on the pistol suddenly got much less casual. His eyes flitted to the firearm then back to me. He held his palms out.

"Hold on now. I didn't kill Peter and I don't see how my writing would convince you I did." He motioned toward the other office. "I think I'm entitled to see for myself what you're talking about."

I looked toward Marks for permission. He nodded then stood.

"Let's all go take a look."

I stepped to the side to allow the men to walk in front, then I slipped the pistol to my holster and followed them in single file around the desks leading to the back of the adjacent room. When we reached Livingston's office space, Marks and I waited on one side of the desk while Collins strode directly to the cabinets where the files were kept. He opened one then quickly ran his fingers along the tops until he found what he wanted. He jerked the envelope then turned and plopped it on the Livingston's desk.

"Peter Trudeau's file."

Marks reached for it and slid the contents out, flipping pages until he found the one he wanted. He slid it across the desk and tapped the emergency contact section. The big man leaned over the paper then slowly shook his head. "Not my writing." He passed it back.

I looked over Marks's shoulder. It was the same paper and the same writing I'd studied on Thursday afternoon when the clerk named James had pulled it at Marks's request. At that time, James had pulled another file. I rubbed my temples. It was the proof that the writing was the same. What file was it? What was the worker's name? I suddenly looked up.

"Gonzales, Lupe C." I motioned for Collins to pull the envelope. Within a few seconds, it too was laying on the table.

Marks glanced at me then emptied the papers and shuffled through to find the one we'd used as proof. He held it up for only an instant then pushed it to rest beside Peter's paperwork. Collins leaned over with both hands on the desk and studied the writing. He stood straight with a scowl.

"I don't know who is telling you this is my writing, but it ain't."

I leaned forward, my head cocked and a half frown on my face. "Are you saying you weren't the one who filled out the form?"

"That's exactly what I'm saying." He turned and took two steps to the left and reached to pull out another envelope. He slapped it to the table with disgust then leaned back and folded his arms.

Marks and I read the name, COLLINS, JONAS written in dark ink across the top. I frowned. James hadn't been able to find that file. Had it been there the entire time? I glanced to Collins then reached to grasp the envelope in both hands. I pulled the papers out and placed them on the desk beside the others.

The script was flowery and at first glance, identical to the writing on the other papers, but as I ran my fingers down each page for comparison, I began to see small but increasingly obvious discrepancies. Collins's writing was more expressive with wider loops and extravagant curls. The penmanship was close, but not the same. I blinked. Who was lying here? Was it Collins? Had he set this up in advance as proof that he wasn't the murderer?

I took a deep breath. As with my other suspects, I mentally crossed Collins off the list. He hadn't killed Peter. If he had, why save Livingston and me from the fire? With us dead there was no reason for the charade of penmanship comparison. But if it wasn't Collins, then who?

I glanced at the envelope with GONZALES, LUPE C. boldly written at the top. I remembered asking James to find Collins's file, but he'd said it was not there. Why would he have lied to me? I shook my head. I knew why.

I turned to Marks. "Where is James?"

"James who?"

I pointed to the man's desk. "James. The feller who helped us the other day. He pulled this as a sample of Collins's writing."

His eyes opened wide as he turned to the empty desk. "I don't know." He took several steps to the closest man at a desk. "Have you seen James?"

The clerk shook his head as he looked up from under his green eyeshade. He shrugged. "James hasn't been in for a couple of days. Nobody's heard from him."

Marks peered at me with a questioning glance. I nodded. I now had a new suspect.

Chapter 16

Collins stared at me as I ran through what I knew and what I suspected. I turned to him. "Would you please pull James's file?"

He stepped to the cabinets and ran his finger over the tops of the envelopes and I watched him frown in frustration. He started again at the front and searched more slowly. With a deep breath he turned.

"Not here."

The implication was clear and both men looked at me. I stepped to James's desk and sat in the rolling, hard-backed chair while I opened each of the drawers. The bottom drawer held a sheaf of papers. I riffled through them until I found one signed by James. I walked it to Livingston's desk and placed it next to Peter's file. I wasn't surprised that the writing matched perfectly.

I gritted my teeth. James had indicated that Collins's file was not there, but he'd been lying, trying to keep suspicion away from himself. I exhaled in frustration. Since my first encounter with Miss Trudeau, or whatever her name was, I had trusted those I should have suspected and suspected those I should have trusted.

I turned to Marks. "Would James have had access to the ingot room?"

He sighed. "Yes. He was Livingston's most trusted subordinate."

"I see. And the key to the hand carts for moving the ingots?"

He nodded sadly.

I turned to Collins. "I'm sorry I doubted you, but as I said, police work is about identifying suspects and working to determine their guilt or innocence." I rubbed my jaw. "Now, I've got a murderer to catch. Do either of you know anything about James?" I leaned against the desk, suddenly tired.

Both shook their heads so I motioned to the front building with my nose.

"Marks, can I use your carriage to go to town? I need to see the deputy there. Maybe he can give me some information." I pointed toward the infirmary. "While you're having it brought around I'm going to see if Livingston is awake. My guess is that if anyone knows anything about the man, he will." I started to leave but stopped and turned. "What's James's last name?"

"Stevenson."

Doc Marlee glanced up as I stepped through the door. He smiled then pointed to the center of the room. I followed his pointing and was happy to see Livingston sitting on the edge of his bed.

I walked directly over. "Good morning. I was hoping you'd be awake."

The bed groaned when he tried to push to a standing position. I held my hand on his shoulder. "Don't get up." I looked at the next bed where I'd spent the last two days. "In fact, I think I'll take a seat too."

A light cough emerged from his chest and he rubbed his temples. "I thought we were goners for sure." He wiped his mouth. "I'll admit to cursing you and your stupid idea when that smoke filled my lungs."

I rubbed the sheets on the bed. "You and me both. We were lucky we made it out."

"How did that happen? Did someone see the fire?"

"Yes, but you won't believe who."

"Who?"

"Jonas Collins."

Livingston's eyes opened wide. "How can that be? I thought he was the one who locked us in there in the first place."

I shook my head. "Turns out he's not the man."

The bed squeaked again as he turned in the bed to look directly at me. "Then who?"

I removed my hat and held it in my hands. If James had been Livingston's most trusted worker, the news would not be well received. "James Stevenson."

His head snapped at the name. "Not possible. James could never be involved in something like that."

I rubbed my fingers over my hat then looked into Livingston's eyes. "Collins proved to me that he wasn't the killer, and in his proof, it's become plain that James is. Think about it. He was trusted and had full access to the ingot room. No one thought twice if he was there. He knew how to move the gold and knew you kept the key to the two wheeled carts in your desk drawer."

"I can't believe it."

"It's a big rock to swallow." I motioned toward the outside. "And he hasn't shown up for work since we got locked in the room."

Livingston sucked air into the side of his mouth. His shoulders slumped in disappointment as he studied the floor. At length, he lifted his face. "He was a good worker, always there early and he stayed late. He told me he was going to Denver soon to marry his fiancé. He had such high hopes for the future."

I frowned, wondering if Miss Trudeau was his intended, then decided that she likely was. I shook my head as I thought of how she'd wrapped me around her little finger then wondered if she'd done the same to him. I pushed up from the bed to stand on the smooth wood floor.

"I'm going to find him. What can you tell me about where he lived, where he went, who were his friends or anything else you can think of?"

He took a deep breath and spoke quietly. "He lived in the middle of town above the bakery. He was single and only needed a bed. He spent most of his time here at the smelter. I don't know any more, other than he was a good employee."

I could feel the regret oozing out of Livingston.

Not regret for anything he'd personally done, but regret for bringing James to work at the smelter, and I questioned again if perhaps it had been Miss Trudeau who'd been the mastermind of the whole affair.

"I'll start tracking him right away." I took a step toward the door. "The sooner I can start, the better." With that, I turned and walked into the bright sunshine.

Marks's carriage with the matched team of bays waited in front of the veranda. The same driver from our first visit smiled and motioned for me to climb in. I took the seat next to him and he wasted no time in coaxing the team into a comfortable trot toward town. He leaned back and placed one boot on the front rail, content to drive in silence. I appreciated that, for I had some thinking to do.

My first stop was the livery stable. As the driver pulled the horses to a stop, the owner stepped out, holding his hand to his forehead to shade his eyes. When he recognized me, he marched close.

"I was hoping you'd show up. I ought to tan your hide for wrecking my buggy and treating my little mare the way you did."

I held my hands out. "I'm sorry about your mare and your buggy. Somebody tried to kill me and stole the cart. If there was any mistreatment, it wasn't me."

He calmed slightly and I was happy to see it. I stepped to the dirt to stand in front of him. "Tell me what happened."

"You were supposed to be back Thursday afternoon and when you didn't show up I figured, with you being a U.S. Marshal and all, that maybe you were on a case and couldn't get back. Then early

Friday morning a ranching family from south of town led the little mare back to me and said the buggy had slid down a ravine close to the river and was broke up bad. They unhooked the mare and brought her in. She'd been out there all night. She had rolled through some cactus and I spent most of the morning pulling thorns out of her." He spat into the dust in remembered anger before looking back to me.

"At that point in time I assumed you were out there somewhere too, so me and Jasper, my occasional hired hand, skedaddled out there to see what we could find. Just like the folks said, the buggy was smashed bad, having tumbled down the ravine. We looked for you but couldn't find a thing."

I leaned against the front wheel so I could see the driver. "Recon you could drive us to take a look?"

"Sure can. Marks told me to stay with you all day if need be."

I turned to the livery man and pointed to the back seat. "Will you show us where?"

He nodded then climbed in. "Take the south road toward the smelter."

The bays trotted at a good clip. We passed the smelter and stayed on the main road south. After some three miles, the livery man tapped the driver on the shoulder and pointed toward the San Pedro River on our left.

"Right there."

In a gully below, I could see the left side wheels of the buggy sticking into the air and one was turning slowly in the breeze. We stopped and got out to stand on the bank and look down at the wreckage. The buggy lay on its side, broken beyond repair, and I could see where the mare had stood through the night on a barren spot between three huge prickly pear cactus plants.

I thought of the three hundred pound ingot. If it had gone over with the buggy, it was probably still there because it was too heavy for James to move by himself. I turned to the livery man. "Mind if I go down and have a look around?"

"Suit yourself, but if you're looking for someone, we already looked."

"Not someone, something." I picked out a trail of sorts through the surprisingly thick prickly pear. I held the front wheel with my left hand while I studied the marks left by the buggy as it careened down the embankment. I stepped closer before I saw what I had been looking for. Marks in the sand and clay showed where James had tried to drag the ingot, but he'd only been able to move it a couple of feet. I climbed through the cactus, carefully choosing my way, to the ingot. It lay partially concealed with dirt and brush. James had tried to hide it with the obvious plan to return at a later time.

I glanced to the men on the road. "Would you men mind giving me a hand?"

They looked at each other, then made their way down the steep, cactus-covered ravine to where I stood. Both men's eyes opened wide when they saw the ingot. They looked at me with questioning expressions. I could understand. It's not often a man gets a chance to be that close to almost a hundred-thousand dollars in gold.

"A gold ingot that was stolen from the smelter." I pointed to the wagon. "There's a good chance that's what caused the buggy to roll down the gully. Too heavy and going too fast. When he couldn't make the turn, the ingot caused the buggy to tip and roll into the gully."

"Yeah. Dragging my little mare with it."

I nodded. "Unfortunately so. I hope she'll be all right."

The driver reached to grasp two of the small ears located on each corner. He heaved but the ingot moved only a few inches. "Oh my!"

I reached to touch him on the arm. "It's almost three hundred pounds. I'm hoping the three of us can get it back up the hill and returned to the smelter. Shall we give it a try?"

Each of us grabbed an ear and together we slid it to an open area. The exertion was too much for me in my weakened state. I coughed long and hard with my hands on my knees and when I wiped my mouth with my sleeve, I saw blood there.

The driver saw it too. "Say, friend. You'd best take it easy."

I cleared my throat. It pained me to admit it, but my strength had waned as a result of the smoke. I clucked my tongue. "Yep. Let's leave this here and get word to Mr. Marks to send some men down to retrieve it." I stood and took as deep a breath as I dared. "But now that the ingot has been found, I need to track down a killer." I waved toward the broken buggy. "He had to walk from here. My guess is that he climbed back to the road to make his escape. Trouble is that after this much time and traffic, there's no telling which way he went."

The men nodded in agreement so I pointed to the top. "If you don't mind, take me to see the deputy."

The ride back to town gave me a chance for

much needed rest. When we pulled to a stop in front of the sheriff's office, I stepped from the buggy then reached to shake the livery man's hand. "I'm sorry again about what happened to the buggy and the mare. If you'll give me a bill, I'll see what I can do to have Colonel Marcomb pay for it."

He waved me off. "I have a better idea. I'll send the bill to the smelting company. After all, they'll be getting the ingot back. If not for the broken buggy, there's no telling where the gold would have wound up."

I smiled. That was good thinking. I'd made the offer but in truth, I had little hope that Marcomb would be able to come up with any money. "Good luck." I turned to the driver. "I'll be all right from here on out. I appreciate your help. Would you please tell Mr. Marks about the ingot and show his men where it is?"

"I'll do that." He paused and looked me up and down. "You're about done in, friend. Take my advice and rest up some before you go traipsing all over the country looking for the killer. You'll never find him if you kill yourself trying."

I was getting sick and tired of people telling me to take it easy. If I heard that one more time I might have to wade in and scramble some brains just to show I could. But in the back of my head, I knew he was right. Trouble was that time was running out. Every hour I stayed in Benson was an hour for James to get farther away. Still, the driver had a point. It wouldn't do for me to run across the fugitive if I was too weak to make an arrest. I reached for a shake. "Thanks. I promise I won't start until tomorrow."

He smiled then slapped the reins to the bays.

"Giddup."

I watched for only a moment before stepping to the boardwalk and into the sheriff's office. The deputy looked up as I entered.

"Well, well. I wondered when you'd show up again. I heard you had a little set to with a fire in the smelter." He motioned for me to take the ladder-backed chair.

The wooden chair groaned as I sat and leaned back. I was exhausted and felt like I could sleep for another two days. I rubbed my hands and coughed again. "Yep. Barely got out alive."

"I'm happy to hear that." He cocked his head. "But you've got some explaining to do. You stop the train and bring back a gold ingot and a dead woman. Don't you think it's about time you told me what in Sam Hill is going on?"

I slid further down in the chair, crossed my ankles and rested my hands on my thighs. It was time to lay all the cards on the table. I clucked my tongue and looked at the deputy with a sigh. "The dead woman I turned over to you when I brought back the train is the key to everything. I assume you took care of her."

He nodded. "Yes. We buried her yesterday morning. Didn't even know her name."

I rubbed my hands on my pants. "I don't know her name either. She told me her name was Trudy Trudeau, but I'm sure that is not her real name. She was in league with a feller by the name of James Stevenson. It appears they were engaged. Anyway, they set out to steal a gold ingot from the smelter, but with the security, it was impossible to get it out of the ingot room." I shook my head. "The plan was elaborate but deadly. They killed a big man for the sole purpose of having a casket available to steal the gold, then Miss Trudeau shows up to take the body back to Santa Fe." I took a deep breath. "The body wasn't in the casket, the gold was. That's when I jumped on your horse and chased the train, but you know about that."

He folded his arms and cocked he head. "I do. You brought her and the ingot back. So how did you get into a fire?"

"Livingston and I got locked in a back room. I had to start a fire hoping someone would notice and save us." The thought of the smoke caused me to cough again. I shuddered as I remembered our time in the room and the fire that almost claimed two more victims for the murderer. I also remembered the deputy's big bay and the breakneck ride to catch the train, and the rifle shot at the saloon. I had brushed against death too many times in the last few days, and I knew that until I had James Stevenson in jail, my duel with the grim reaper would go on. James had killed an innocent man in cold blood simply because of his size, so I had no hope that he would give himself up without a fight, but I had to find him first.

I wiped the corners of my mouth with my thumb and finger. "Lucky for us someone found us. Then this morning we located the overturned buggy in a gully south of town. The smelter men will be there soon to recover the ingot and get it back to the smelter."

He chuckled. "So you lost it, then found it and took it back, only to lose it again."

I frowned. I admitted to myself that this case had not been one of my most brilliant. I'd been charmed by the woman and blinded by my feelings for her. I vowed never to make that mistake again. I glanced to the deputy. "I suppose. But it's been found again and will soon be in its rightful place."

He listened patiently, then whistled low. "And now you're convinced this here Stevenson feller was the man on the inside?"

It was a soul-searching question. This investigation had been far from ordinary. As I identified suspects, I'd been fairly certain as to the guilt of Livingston, Collins and even Marks during different stages of my stay. But with the increasing evidence, I had no doubt that Stevenson was the culprit.

I looked into the deputy's gray eyes. "Yes, sir."

"And he was the one who locked you in the room?"

I tapped the desk, feeling foolish that we'd been trapped. "He was. I'm sure of it."

The deputy ran a finger inside his collar while tilting his head back and forth. "Then what do you want from me?"

I paused. That was a fair question. What did I want from him? I recognized my physical weakness and would have to work within my limits. I wondered for only a second about asking him to take over the investigation, but the thought was fleeting and immediately discarded. I was a U.S. Marshal and I'd get Stevenson no matter how long it took. I rubbed my face then looked up. "Only information. Do you know anything about James Stevenson?"

He leaned back and scratched the stubble on his jaw. "Can't say as I do. Other than the fact that he lived above the bakery. I saw him now and again in town, but we never spoke that I can remember."

I pinched the bridge of my nose. "I'm sure he's long gone from here."

The chair squeaked when he leaned back and placed his feet on the desk. He clasped his hands over his belt and studied me.

"What?" My frown deepened.

His smile was humorless. "He may be gone, but there's another possibility."

I sat up in the chair and leaned forward. "What's that?"

"Do you think it's possible he never left, but will wait for a chance to put a bullet in you, the man who recovered the ingot and killed his fiancé."

"I didn't kill his fian—." I breathed deeply, realizing that as tired as I was I hadn't thought that that the man might try to kill me. I remembered the shots fired at me near the saloon a few nights earlier and knew Stevenson was capable of ambush. "You might have a point. I'll watch my back."

"You do that. In the meantime, what's next?"

The legs of the chair screeched on the board floor as I pushed to my feet. "I'd like to take a look inside James Stevenson's room above the bakery."

The deputy stood and reached for his ten-gallon hat on the rack at the wall. He mashed it on his head while pacing to the door. "Let's go."

I followed the bigger man stride for stride, but by the time we got across the street and onto the boardwalk, I had to stop and rest. My breathing was heavy as I leaned with hands on knees and head hanging. A deep fit of coughing exploded from my chest. When it subsided, I spat a glob of blood to the street.

"Marshal Hawk, you're in a bad way. Why don't you go to the hotel and rest while I look around? I'll fill you in on anything I find."

I shook my head. "I'll be all right." I straightened and pointed to the wooden stairs at the side of the building. "Shall we go?"

He raised his eyebrows, then turned and grabbed the railing and started up, his heavy boots clunking on the thick boards. I followed at a slower pace and leaned on the rails at the top landing. My breath came is gasps at the exertion and it seemed as though I couldn't get enough air. The deputy studied me with an expression of concern, but I shook my head at his unspoken apprehension. I stood straight, pulled my pistol and used it to motion for him to open the door.

He twisted the knob. It turned easily in his hand and the hinges creaked as the door swung inward. We both looked inside, and after seeing no one there, I holstered my gun and followed the deputy into the room.

Chapter 17

It was a small room, neat and well-kept with only a bed against one wall and a roll-top writing desk against another. I stepped directly to the desk and sat in the small, wooden chair. I pushed the top up in a smooth motion. It clattered as it retracted into whatever space it went to, then my full concentration was on the desktop. It was bare except for an inkwell at the corner and a bound book next to it. I slid the book closer and opened it to see ledger pages with neatly written entries. I saw nothing there of any interest so I opened the top drawer where I saw, among other things, pencils, odds and ends and a sheaf of blank writing paper. It looked much like the top drawer of my desk in

Tucson where I placed anything I might collect from my pockets. I pushed the drawer closed then tried those on the side. The top drawer was locked and I jerked my head to look at the deputy. He shrugged, but I had a thought. I slowly opened the top drawer again and rummaged through the collection of things there. Pencils and quill pens, three bullets for a .44, a washer and a few scraps of paper.

Finally, I saw the key. As expected, it slid into the hole and when I turned it, the lock clicked. I smiled smugly while pulling the handle. My eyes opened wide when I saw the contents and I was thankful for the man's bookkeeping mindset. Neatly stacked papers rested in two piles. The first identical to the blank papers on the top drawer and the second pile contained correspondence torn from a telegraph pad. I lifted both piles and placed them on the desktop.

As in Marks's office a few nights earlier, the papers were carefully arranged from the most recent message on top. I pulled the first page of received messages on the telegraph paper written in neat, blocky letters.

JAMES STEVENSON, BENSON, ARIZONA TERRITORY

IN DEMING. BE THERE TOMORROW. KATIE

I turned to the next page dated one day earlier.

JAMES STEVENSON, BENSON, ARIZONA TERRITORY

RECEIVED MESSAGE TO WAIT FOR TELEGRAPH IN SANTA FE FOR T. TRUDEAU. ALL PREPARATIONS IN PLACE. WILL LEAVE TOMORROW. KATIE

I pulled the first of the handwritten messages

with flowering script that I recognized as James Stevenson. There was no date.

KATIE STROUD, DENVER, COLORADO

EXPECT MESSAGE FROM MARKS TO T. TRUDEAU IN SANTA FE WITHIN WEEK. RESPOND IMMEDIATELY TO HOLD BROTHER. ALL PROCEEDING AS PLANNED. BE CAREFUL. JAMES

I didn't need to see more. I knew the story and I'd been a big part of it. I looked up to the deputy who'd been reading over my shoulder.

He leaned back. "No doubt now."

I grunted. "I'm sure when...," I looked at the name on the messages, "Katie Stroud was safely away, James was planning on coming back here to destroy these."

"I'm sure you're right. Everything was too meticulously planned to leave those papers as a loose end."

I nodded then flipped through both piles to see if there was anything of interest. James had regularly communicated with Katie over the past year but other than messages sent and received about planned trips to see one another, there were no additional messages concerning stealing the gold.

I lifted the top few papers from each pile and handed them to the deputy. "You keep these as evidence. I'll track the man down and bring him back." I slapped my knee and stood, but the quick movement was more than my weakened body could stand. I swayed and fell.

I opened my eyes to see the deputy kneeling over me and slapping my face. He stopped and leaned back when he saw my awakening.

"Marshal, you need to get some rest." He

reached for my hand to pull me to a sitting position.

I was slowly coming to the realization that the smoke had taken more out of me than I thought, and it didn't help that in my haste to get to the bottom of this case, I hadn't eaten since the day before. I held my head in my hands and rubbed above my eyes.

He stood and offered me his hand again, then slowly pulled me to my feet. He stood close until I waved him away.

"I hate to admit it but you might be right. Maybe another day in the infirmary might do me good, but first can we go to Carlita's and get a bite to eat?"

He opened the door and held it as I stepped out to the landing. I held tightly to the railing to keep from falling again. When we finally reached the bottom, I rested before pointing forward with my nose.

"Shall we?"

The smell of stew and bread made my mouth water. I took a seat on the long bench and nodded when Carlita brought the bowl and splatted a generous helping of stew to my plate, then did the same for the deputy. I leaned both elbows on the table, then, with a metal spoon in one hand and a fat slice of bread in the other, I ate.

Three helpings later, I leaned back and patted my stomach. I may have been weak but my appetite was still intact. The meal had been just what I'd needed. I rested my face in my hands and yawned. The deputy leaned to my ear.

"You are dead on your feet. Let's get you to the sheriff's office where you can sleep in one of the cells." We walked back to the Sheriff's Office with my eyelids growing heavier by the minute.

My eyes opened slowly and as I looked at the board ceiling, I wondered where I was. I turned my head slightly against the rough cloth of the pillow at my neck and the rougher wool of the blanket at my throat. When I saw the bars, I remembered the deputy mentioning sleep in a cell, but I don't know how I got there. The bed groaned as I rolled to a sitting position.

The iron bar door gaped open and I was happy to see it. I hated jail cells, especially when I was on the inside. I leaned forward but I could see no one in the darkened office. I glanced over my shoulder and noticed the small window high on the rock wall. From where I sat, I could see stars in the night sky. I rolled my head left and right, then with a grunt, wrapped the wool blanket about my shoulders and lay back on the bed. Maybe this cell wasn't so bad after all.

When I next awoke, I squinted at the brightness coming through the open door of the office as well as the window above my head. I breathed deeply and licked my lips at the aroma of brewing coffee. I rolled my feet to the floor as I sat on the bed, then I heard what I hoped was the sound of hot coffee being poured into a metal cup.

I heard the unmistakable clang of the pot being replaced to the potbellied stove, then the deputy appeared. He smiled when he saw me and raised one of the cups he carried in greeting.

"Good afternoon."

I sat straight. "Afternoon?"

He chuckled. "Yep. You slept a full twenty-four hours." He held a cup toward me.

I took it by the handle and held it on my knee

while I looked up into his jovial face.

"Twenty four hours?"

"Yep."

I yawned, then rubbed my face with my free hand. I was starving and I knew that had to be a good sign. I blew across the coffee, intrigued with the ripples on the black liquid. I took a sip and discovered it was hot, but not excessively so. I held the cup toward him in thanks, then sipped again. "Obliged."

He shrugged then motioned for me to join him at the desk.

I stood and stretched with one hand high over my head. It was a wonder what a good meal and a full day's sleep could do for a man. I patted my stomach. One more meal like the one I'd had the day before and I'd be as good as new. The deputy sat and put his feet on the desk while I took the seat to the front.

I placed my cup on the desk, slouched in the ladder-back chair and crossed my legs. He watched me with his head cocked and a small smile.

"Looks like you're feeling a sight better."

"I am. Thanks for letting me sleep." I waved toward the outside. "Anything new since yesterday?"

He took a long sip of the coffee. "No. I took the liberty to ask around about James Stevenson, but no one knew much. It seems he had no friends here in town to speak of. From what I gather, he spent all his time at the smelter, and when he wasn't there he stayed in his room."

I leaned to slide my cup onto the desk then rubbed the back of my neck while moving my head from side to side. "That's the impression I got when I talked to Livingston. He said Stevenson was a good worker. I'm not altogether sure he agrees with me that the man was the thief."

The deputy leaned forward and let his boots fall to the floor with a thump. He reached to grasp the papers on his desk. "He'll have no doubt once he reads these."

I nodded and raised my eyebrows as I recognized the papers we'd taken from James's room. "That's the truth." I looked again at the yellowed, telegraph paper he held toward me. I leaned forward to read the words as though for the first time.

JAMES STEVENSON, BENSON, ARIZONA TERRITORY

RECEIVED MESSAGE TO WAIT FOR TELEGRAPH IN SANTA FE FOR T. TRUDEAU. ALL PREPARATIONS IN PLACE. WILL LEAVE TOMORROW. KATIE

I slapped my forehead with my palm. The emergency contact! He would have listed someone and I needed to know who that someone was. He may not have had any friends in town, but he would have listed someone, and that someone may be the key to his whereabouts. I stood, immediately happy that the movement caused no dizziness. I would get something to eat soon, but I had to make my way to the smelter right away. "Deputy, you wouldn't happen to have your bay horse close by would you?"

He stood with a puzzled expression. "Tied to the rail in the back. I always keep him saddled when I'm here in case something comes up."

I turned and ran through the door and to the back of the small building. The bay raised his head, somewhat surprised at my sudden approach. His eyes opened wide and he cocked his head, but he made no effort to shy away. I pulled the slipknot and stepped into the saddle. Leaning forward, I pushed the horse into a trot until we reached the street, then with a quick wave to the bewildered deputy standing and watching from the boardwalk, I kicked the bay into an all-out run.

I slid the bay to a stop in front of the infirmary then dismounted and tossed the reins over a rail at the front of the building. In two quick steps I reached the door and pushed it inward. Doc Marlee and Livingston looked up from a table at the far side of the room. Each had a white cloth tucked into their shirts under their chins and the table appeared piled high with food. I strode directly to them.

The doc pointed to a chair before reaching for an empty plate and spoon, which he placed directly in front of me as I sat. "You're just in time." He pushed a bowl of beef and beans toward me, and Livingston passed half of a broken loaf of bread.

"Thanks." I ladled the beef and beans onto my plate and took a huge bite. I had important business to attend to, but I also needed to keep my strength up. And I'd learned long ago to eat when I had a chance. After swallowing, I looked to Livingston. "I came to see who the emergency contact for James Stevenson was. His file was gone, but I'm hoping there is something in his desk that would indicate who he listed. That might give me a clue as to his whereabouts." I took another bite.

He waved toward the offices across the courtyard. "I'm planning on heading over there as soon as we eat."

I nodded. "Then let's get after it. I have a murderer to catch." I then ate my fill.

Livingston squinted as we exited the infirmary.

It was obvious this was his first attempt to be outside since the fire. He moved slowly, slightly bent at the waist, and his wheezing breath told me he was in much worse shape than I was. We walked through the open area, then he stopped to rest, leaning on the wall at the main office entrance door. A sudden cough, hard and hacking, caused him to double over with his hands on his knees.

I held his shoulders to keep him from falling. When the attack passed, he breathed shallowly, then looked up.

"Thanks."

I felt guilty that the fire I'd started had hurt the man. "I'm sorry, Livingston. Maybe the fire wasn't the best idea."

He shook his head. "Don't apologize. Something needed to be done, and you did it. If not, we would have died in there."

What he said was true, but he would likely have to live with the consequences of the hot smoke the rest of his life. Still, I realized, at least he had the rest of his life to live.

I held the door then followed him toward his office space. When we got there, several of the clerks stood and welcomed him back. He waved them off then sat heavily in his chair, his breathing coming in painful gasps.

All the clerks returned to their desks except one who stood holding a folded paper. He looked from Livingston to me then back again.

"Mr. Livingston, sir?"

"Yes?"

"James Stevenson stopped by early yesterday. I noticed he hadn't been to work for a few days so I welcomed him and told him it was good to have him back while you were in the infirmary."

I jerked my head at the mention of the murderer. "James Stevenson?"

He looked at me and swallowed hard. "Yes." He turned his attention to Livingston. "But he said he didn't work here anymore. The clerk slid the paper across the desk toward Livingston. "He said to give you this."

In bold, block letters, my name was written across the folded paper. I reached and quickly jerked it away from Livingston's outstretched hand. I hurriedly unfolded it to read: YOU KILLED KATIE. YOU'RE A DEAD MAN.

Without conscious thought, I looked out the window to the smelter, noticing the black smoke drifting lazily in the breeze. It was clear that James had not left town, but as the deputy had suggested, he'd stayed to put a bullet in me. I thought of my night stay in the jail and decided that it had allowed me some much-needed rest, but also had taken the chance for an ambush away from the killer. I frowned at Livingston.

He looked at me with his head cocked. "Well?"

I passed the paper over. He read it and shook his head before turning to the clerk.

"Did James say where he was headed?"

"Nope."

I impatiently tapped the desk. "Let's find something that will tell us where he is?"

Livingston coughed and looked to the clerk. "Would you excuse us please?"

After he was gone, Livingston took a deep breath. "I'm the emergency contact."

I snapped my head and leaned forward. "What?"

His shoulders sagged and the chair squeaked when he leaned back. I watched his knuckles turn white at the fierce gripping of the chair arms. I waited but my patience was growing thin.

Livingston glanced up. His lips pursed and I could see his jaw muscles working under his skin. He looked defeated. "All right. It was bound to come out sooner or later. I'm the one who hired James. We grew up together in a mining town in northern Nevada. When I got the job as the head bookkeeper here at the smelter, I needed a right hand man. Stevenson learned fast and was quick to take on any assignment. He soon knew more about the operation than I did, but as far as I knew, he was always one hundred percent honest. That's the reason I was so adamant that he couldn't be involved in the killing and theft."

I nodded because it made sense, but I was not quite ready to leave it lay. "Anything else?"

He scanned around nervously while drumming his fingers on the chair arm. "He changed after he got engaged. I never met the woman, but he talked about her all the time. He started spending more time in the smelter and ingot room. I didn't think anything of it. He was a good employee and the more he did, the better it was for me."

"Let me guess. He suddenly became interested in how the ingots were made and moved?"

Livingston sighed. "Yes. At the time it seemed so natural."

"How about now?"

He looked at me with a stricken face. Finally, he held his head in his hands and leaned his elbows on the desk. He took a shallow breath, then glanced at me over the tops of his fingers. "Now the reasons for doing what he did are obvious. I can see how he planned everything." His eyes bored into me. "But you have to believe me that I had nothing to do with the theft." He sat up straighter. "I can't imagine what got into him."

Chapter 18

I could imagine what got into him. Her name was Katie Stroud, or Miss Trudeau as I'd known her. I'd seen firsthand what she was capable of and I had no doubt that she had worked on him until he agreed to carry out the plan. And I had to admit that it had been a good plan, one that, except for a nagging suspicion on my part, would have succeeded. I had a sudden, morbid thought. What was Miss Trudeau's eventual goal? Would she have disappeared with the gold, never to see James again? I breathed deeply. Or worse, would she have killed him as she surely would have killed me in the baggage car if I hadn't pulled the brake cord? I shook my head. The love for a woman can make a man do things they never would have otherwise considered.

I let out a breath. I believed him for the simple reason that if Livingston was involved, he never would have told me about the missing ingot when I first arrived.

He leaned back in the chair and folded his arms. "I'm sorry, Marshal Hawk. I should have told you when you first suggested he was the thief, but I couldn't bring myself to believe that he had stooped so low."

I leaned back and interlaced my fingers, then held my thumbs under my chin and my knuckles over my lips. I closed my eyes, remembering what James looked like. I would need to act fast if I saw him, although my suspicion was that he'd ambush me long distance with a rifle. It was not a pleasant thought. I cocked my head and opened my eyes, peering at the remorseful face across the desk.

"Do you know where he might be now?"

He shook his head. "I'd tell you if I knew. Nothing would please me more." His eyes opened wide at my frown and he leaned forward. "That's the honest truth. I don't know where he is."

I stood and walked to the big windows behind Livingston's desk. I looked absently at the smelter buildings while I thought about my next move. I'd have to be attentive to every possibility, but that was unrealistic. Stevenson could hide anywhere, then reach out with a rifle and fill me with a .44 slug. I refused to live in constant fear, always looking over my shoulder, wondering where he was and when he would take his shot. I needed to be on the offensive. I wouldn't let him hunt me, I'd hunt him.

I looked toward the wood yard when a sudden

movement accompanied by a metallic glint caught my attention. Out of instinct, I dropped to the floor immediately before the window where I'd stood crashed inward. I bounced to my feet with gun drawn and took two quick but ineffective shots through the broken window at the shooter who ran, pistol in hand, toward the smelter.

I rushed the door and threw it open and sprinted in chase, but after only thirty yards my chest burned and a coughing fit doubled me over. As soon as I was able, I resumed my chase, but at a much slower pace. Stevenson had disappeared through the ore wagon doors so I jogged there, changing directions left and right to prevent an easy shot. I stopped at the big door, hiding behind the huge timbers as much as possible while cautiously peering to the darkened interior.

The heat poured from the opening and I could see the smelter was in full operation, with men at work at their various tasks. I ignored those without shirts but scrutinized the others. I saw no sign of James Stevenson. I glanced at the tower in hopes of seeing Old Moses or Collins there, but the platform was empty. I coughed again and swallowed hard. I was in no position to chase the man, my only hope was to keep him inside and get into a position to take him prisoner, or, kill him before he killed me. I took a breath then ran with measured steps through the workers on the smelter floor. They stopped to look at me with my pistol at the ready. I recognized the fire tenders and while hiding behind a pillar, motioned for them to join me. I recognized the one called Pablo, who I'd spoken to earlier. He walked close then stood next to me, eyeing my gun with a puzzled expression.

"Pablo, have you seen James Stevenson?"

He wiped the sweat from his face then pointed to the darkness of the ingot room. "He was here a minute ago. He went down the stairs."

I nodded my appreciation, already intent on how I might get down the stairs without a bullet in my chest. I moved from pillar to pillar until I was scarcely feet from the handrail. I swallowed hard, knowing that I would be silhouetted on the landing by the light from the huge ore wagon doors behind me. With a deep breath, I rushed forward, taking the steps two at a time while hoping I didn't stumble as the light grew dimmer. A shot sounded and I felt the whap of the bullet pass my ear, but in two more steps I was at the bottom.

The gleam of the gold ingots stacked neatly waiting for the next shipment caught my attention. I squatted behind them for protection and took a moment to replace the two spent shells in my gun. Keeping my head down as much as possible I looked over the top ingots and searched for any movement. I didn't know exactly where his shot had come from because of the echo bouncing back from the walls. And I'd been so intent on watching the steps as I ran, I hadn't been able to see any flash from the gun. What I did know, or at least I hoped I knew, was that the loading door that could be seen from Livingston's office was locked. If that was the case, Stevenson was trapped, for the only way out was the stairs at my back.

I cupped my hand alongside my mouth and yelled. "Give yourself up, James. There's no way out."

I heard another shot, accompanied by the indescribable sound of a bullet striking the soft gold ingots. I snapped a shot of my own toward the flash of his gun, but knew I'd missed. I waited with eyes closed, intent on any sound he might make, anything to tell me where he was or where he was heading, but I could hear nothing over the noise of the furnace and the work going on in the smelter only forty feet from the top of the stairs above me. I wondered if anyone there had heard the gunshots and decided they probably had not.

I placed my left hand on the gold, surprised that the ingots seemed cool to the touch compared to the warm air. I licked my lips and yelled into the darkness. "Turn yourself in, James."

"I don't think so."

I tried to get a bearing on his location, but the noise from above was too great. I rested my gun hand on the ingot stack with my pistol pointed in his general direction. "It's in your best interest."

"I don't care what happens to me. You killed Katie and I'm going to kill you."

"James, I know what you felt. Katie pulled me in too. She had a way. She knew what she was doing. You aren't a thief, James. You only did it because she made you."

"You're a liar. You didn't know her like I did. She was the sweetest girl. I wanted to get us a start. The smelter wouldn't miss one ingot. They ship millions of dollars a month and paid me almost nothing. I deserved more. It took me a year to convince her to help me get the gold out."

I cocked my head. Was he so distraught that he thought the theft was his idea, that he was the mastermind? I ruminated on his words and felt the beginnings of a hope that Miss Trudeau was the pawn in the whole affair and not the queen. "Are you telling me you planned the theft, not her?"

"That's right. She was against it from the start. She finally agreed, but only if I promised that no one would get hurt."

I thought of her comments in the baggage car of how she'd tried to distance herself from me, but that I had refused to leave. I quickly ran through our conversations and saw, to my dismay, that she had told the truth. I had been the one who, over and over, had forced myself into her company. She had not manipulated me, had not made me accompany her, had not made me into an unwitting accomplice to the theft. I felt foolish at the recognition of my gullibility, but somehow that didn't seem to matter because of the excitement and relief that flooded into my chest at learning that Miss Trudeau was not as evil as I'd come to believe. I leaned my forehead against an ingot, enjoying the coolness against my skin. I couldn't keep the smile from my face and I wanted to shout for joy. Instead of a dastardly villain who thought only of herself, I had fallen in love with a poor, misguided girl who had opposed the plan from the beginning. She'd only gone along out of love for James.

My mind wrapped around something Stevenson said about not hurting anyone. In the freight car, she'd mentioned that Peter's death was an accident, I now believed she had thought that to be true. I raised my face. "You promised that no one would get hurt, but you killed Peter?"

"I couldn't wait for an accident. He was big and I needed a big man who weighted the same as an ingot."

"So you lied to Katie?"

"It had to be done." He shot again, putting two bullets into the ingot stack.

All thoughts of Miss Trudeau vanished and I turned my complete attention to the killer. I returned fire, pulling my trigger four times, putting a slug at the center of his muzzle flash, one each left and right and one down low. I was confident that at least one of the shots had hit their mark, unless, of course, he was more experienced than I expected and had moved rapidly away after shooting.

I reloaded while waiting for another shot. When it did not come, I pushed away to slowly move along the breastwork of timbers which made up the retaining wall between the two levels. I would make my way to where he was, but I would approach from a different direction. He could be dead or possibly wounded, or perhaps he'd moved enough after shooting to escape unscathed.

After twenty silent steps toward the center of the pitch-black room, I stopped and took a knee on the powdery dust of the floor. As near as I could tell, I should have been close to where he'd fired his shots. If I'd hit him, he would not be far. I felt for a body with my hand as I crawled on my knees. At length I squatted on my heels as I came to the understanding that my shots had been fruitless and that he continued to hunt me. I turned my head back and forth, listening for any sound. I hoped to hear something because the din of the smelter noise diminished as I got farther into the room. I looked to my left and could see the two portholes where Livingston had tried to call Juan while we were locked in the room, but the tiny amount of light they provided was useless. To my right, a small shaft of light penetrated dimly into the room from the space between the ingot room loading door and the frame.

In sudden thought, I realized he had been in this room countless time and knew it much better than I did. Was there another way out? A small door that I knew nothing about? Was that the reason he had decided to enter in the first place? I looked back to the base of the huge smokestack in the smelter area and wiped the sweat from my eyes. My only choice was to go on the offensive. The darkness would hide me as well as it was hiding him. I stood with a deep breath.

A shadow crossed in front of the sliver of light from the loading door. It was gone before I could fire, but I knew where he was. That gave me a distinct advantage. I jogged as quietly as possible toward the edge of the rock wall opposite the door, careful not to venture too close to the burned debris. I couldn't afford to trip and give my location away. I stopped and waited, confused as to where he was going and why.

The more he moved toward the farthest point from the smelter, the further he was from any possibility of escape. It didn't make sense.

My head snapped in instant clarity. His movement had nothing to do with escape, but everything to do with drawing me into an ambush.

From the edge of the building farthest from the smelter, a sudden shaft of bright light flooded into the big room. I turned in time to glimpse Stevenson rushing through an open door. I snapped a quick shot and saw the wood of the doorjamb explode, but the man was already through. I ran to the long rectangle of light, huddling close to the door in relative darkness. Without exposing my head, I looked out.

It was an enclosure or corral of some type and

I concluded that Juan and his father had used the rock wall of the building as one side of their corral. I could see rough-cut boards closely nailed to the perimeter, and the ground between the ingot room and the outside fence was devoid of any plant growth. Obviously, the small burro had eaten every blade of grass or weed that might have had a chance to grow there. I backtracked, making a hurried trip around the rectangle of light so I could approach the door from the opposite side.

I stared into the light, taking time for my eyes to adjust. My fear was that Stevenson waited, barely out of sight, ready to pump lead into me as fast as he could pull the trigger the moment I stepped through the door. My only advantage was surprise. My hope was that I could rush out, locate and shoot him before he could shoot me, but my eyes would have to be acclimated to the bright sunshine.

"What are you waiting for marshal?"

I listened without answering, trying to get a bearing on where he might be.

"You are brave when it comes to killing women, but how about facing a man. Say your prayers, then come on out and meet your executioner."

From the sound I was almost certain he stood, with gun ready, against the rock wall no more than fifteen feet to the left of the door. I considered my options, but they were few. Of course, I could have turned tail and run, but I wasn't willing to do that. In the first place, it would have been cowardly, and I was no coward. And in the second place, if he escaped now, the time would come when he might wait for me when I least expected. No, I would face the danger like a U.S. Marshal, guns blazing and lead flying.

I jerked my head when I heard a call.

"Hello, señor." It was a boy's voice. I assumed it was Juan. Who else would be there?

I heard a scuffle and a stifled yelp, then the dreaded words, "Marshal, you coward. I know you want to turn and run, but I've got the boy. Come out or I'll put a bullet in him and it will be your fault."

My head dropped. Juan had chosen the absolute worst time to show up. Contrary to what Stevenson might think, I was not going to turn and run. It wasn't my nature. All my life I'd faced hard things and danger, and I'd done it head on. This situation was no different, but I would have to be careful so the boy would not be injured.

"Let the boy go, Stevenson. He has no part of this. It's between me and you and nobody else."

His laugh was cruel and unbalanced. He sounded like a crazy man. "Step on out, marshal. You'll get what's coming to you."

I hefted my pistol, feeling the weight and balance as I thought about what was to come. My best course of action was to charge through, turn and fire while hoping his shot was off target, but that was a mighty big gamble. On top of that, he held Juan. I couldn't let the boy be injured. Although I was willing to take chances with my own life, his was another story. He was an innocent boy in the wrong place at the wrong time.

My only advantage was that Stevenson wouldn't know exactly when I would bolt through the door. That fraction of a second for him to recognize and pull the trigger might be enough. I had confidence in my ability, but the underlying question was his exact location. Almost certain was not enough. A sliver of time searching for him would be the difference between life and death for me and possibly Juan.

Across the way, a black crow sat on the top of the fence, unconcerned, intently studying something close to the wall. It cocked its head, and I was sure he looked directly at James Stevenson. If that was the case, I knew exactly where the murderer stood.

I breathed deeply and swallowed a cough, cursing my healing lungs. I couldn't afford to let the man know where I was, for the element of surprise was the only way I could get out alive and save the boy. Stevenson didn't know the exact moment I would charge through, and I counted on that split second to be the difference. I wiped the sweat from over my eyes then readied for the lunge through the door.

Like a mountain lion after its prey, I bolted into the light. Stevenson stood exactly where I'd expected. He held the boy to his chest and his gun was up. I squeezed my trigger and felt the kick of my gun a fraction of a second before I heard his. My aim had been good, a shot of a lifetime in a lifetime of shots. My bullet entered Stevenson's left eye only inches above Juan's head. He collapsed immediately to the dirt as the lead pierced his brain. Juan screamed as the falling body pulled him down, but I knew he was uninjured, only scared.

In that brief moment, just as after every gunfight I'd ever had, my senses were alive. I noticed everything from the coolness of the winter air mixed with the warmness of the sun on my shoulders. I heard the flapping of the wings and the cawing of the crow as it hurtled skyward, desperately trying to escape the sudden danger. I straightened from my hunched position and took three steps to lift Juan to his feet. He turned and ran for his house, screaming all the way. I watched him retreat, relieved that no harm had come to him. I looked back to Stevenson, crumpled on the packed earth, and I remembered the thief on the train who had stolen Miss Trudeau's purse. That man was the start of getting me into this whole mess in the first place. He had underestimated me and paid for it, and now, Stevenson had done the same, with the same result.

I breathed deeply and a violent coughing spasm gripped my entire body. I dropped to one knee and slowly let the tension flow from me. As I replaced my pistol to its holster, I noticed something trickling down my chest. I pulled my shirt away. I couldn't see a wound, but as I felt my neck, I flinched as my hand ran across a deep crease above my collarbone. Strange, I thought to myself, that there had been no pain. I gingerly felt the gash and moved my arm and shoulder. There was no significant damage and as I stood there, the slight bleeding all but stopped. I looked at the dead man one last time and shook my head. I had survived once again.

I stepped through the door into the darkness of the ingot room and leaned against the wall to catch my breath for a moment. The case was solved and the perpetrators punished. My work in Benson was done. I breathed again then wiped my eyes with my sleeve. No, there was one more thing I wanted to do, but first I had to let Livingston know what had happened.

Doc Marlee fussed over the burn on my neck. He cleaned the wound and painted it with a purple salve that stung like the dickens. The confounded medicine hurt worse than the gash. I waved him away and pulled my shirt back to my shoulders.

"You'd best rest, young man."

I shook my head. "I've rested about all I can stand. I've got to see a man to remind him about a trial, then I'm Tucson bound."

Livingston stepped forward. "Thanks for being here, Marshal." He reached into his drawer and pulled two twenty-dollar gold pieces from a steel box and pressed them into my hand. "For expenses."

I clinked the coins together and nodded as I slipped them into my pocket. "Thanks." I pointed toward Juan's home. "You be sure to check on the boy."

He nodded and clapped me on my back. "Sure thing."

The big bay tugged at the bit, anxious to be home. I let him have his head and he settled into a comfortable lope. At the sheriff's office, I dismounted and threw the reins over the hitching rail before stepping onto the boardwalk.

The deputy met me at the door, then moved inside and pointed to the chair. "You look plumb done in."

I sat heavily. "I feel plumb done in."

"What happened?"

I leaned back in the chair and told the story. When finished, I sat up. "My work here is done, except for one thing."

He leaned forward. "What's that?"

I reached into my pocket to grasp one of the twenty-dollar gold pieces. I placed it on the desk and reached for a pencil and paper. In bold, dark letters I wrote, KATIE STROUD/TRUDY TRUDEAU. I handed it to him and smiled at his puzzled expression. I motioned toward the paper with my nose. "I'd like to have a small headstone placed on the woman's grave. Would you mind taking care of that for me?" I slid the coin across.

He shrugged. "Sure." He read the paper again. "But why two names?"

I pressed my lips together and folded my arms. "Because she was two women, one a thief, but one a lady. I prefer to remember her as Miss Trudeau."

His gray eyes sparkled.

I slapped my thighs as I stood. "When's the next train to Tucson?"

He pulled his pocket watch and smiled. "You're in luck. One leaves in just over an hour."

I easily found the man I'd come to Benson to see. After reminding him of the trial, I strolled to the train station and pushed six bits into the metal bowl under the bars at the ticket window.

"Tucson, please."

The white-headed, mustachioed stationmaster slowly ripped a ticket from a spool and placed it into the same dish. I retrieved it and slid it into my coat pocket then stepped back into the Arizona winter sun. I looked east toward the San Pedro River and saw the approaching train crossing the bridge, the thick, black smoke of the engine trailing for a half mile behind. The train pulled into the station in a cloud of escaping steam and I stepped into the last car. I turned for a final glance at Boot Hill and tipped my hat to Trudy Trudeau, a fine woman who had made the mistake of falling in love with the wrong man. May she rest in peace!

The End

Author's note:

The smelter in Benson operated for only a few years in the early 1880s.

An interesting side note is that when they shipped the processed gold, they didn't bother to send guards even though the shipments contained hundreds of thousands of dollars in almost pure gold. They determined the ingots were too heavy for anyone to steal, and they were right.

Other books by Randall Dale:
Pardner's Trust Series
Pardner's Trust, Cowboy Up
Friends in Deed
Hidden Regrets
A Good Man Gone

Branson Hawk, U.S. Marshal Series
The Wichita Connection
Dead Man's Gold
Beginnings (Coming Soon)

The Captain's Coat
The Posse

Made in the USA
Columbia, SC
11 August 2019